THE WYOMING BUBBLE

Center Point
Large Print

Also by Allan Vaughan Elston and available from Center Point Large Print:

Grand Mesa
Wyoming Manhunt
Showdown
Gun Law at Laramie
Wagon Wheel Gap
Paradise Prairie

THE WYOMING BUBBLE

Allan Vaughan Elston

CENTER POINT LARGE PRINT
THORNDIKE, MAINE

This Center Point Large Print edition
is published in the year 2025 by arrangement with
Golden West Inc.

Copyright © 1955 by Allan Vaughan Elston.
Renewed copyright © 1986 by John William
Elston & Jean Corwin.

All rights reserved.

The text of this Large Print edition is unabridged.
In other aspects, this book may vary
from the original edition.
Printed in the United States of America
on permanent paper sourced using
environmentally responsible foresting methods.
Set in 16-point Times New Roman type.

ISBN: 979-8-89164-458-8

The Library of Congress has cataloged this record
under Library of Congress Control Number: 2024948309

To the old Cheyenne *Leader*—a sleeping history in the archives of Wyoming—from whose files for the year 1883 comes much of the background for this book.

THE WYOMING BUBBLE

1

The shot came from his right and the horse under Hyatt stumbled. It went to its knees, then rolled flank-down to the sod and never got up again. By that time two more bullets had whistled by and Russ Hyatt had his own carbine out of the scabbard. He flattened behind his dying horse and took aim on the great open spaces of Wyoming.

That was all he could see. There was nothing to shoot at except the echoes of three shots. Patches of scrubby greasewood and a few boulders rimmed a rise about two hundred yards to his right. But the morning sunlight raised no glint from a rifle barrel. Russ Hyatt lay prone with his carbine cocked, swinging it in a short slow arc to pick up a target.

Fury boiled inside of him. Because now Tony, his sorrel horse, had stopped quivering. It was a head hit and the horse was dead—dead from a bullet meant for Russ himself. Russ had no idea why he'd been shot at and right now was too mad to speculate about it. His eyes kept searching for something to shoot at—shoulder or hatted head or steel barrel—but the rise of ground showed nothing except greasewood and rock and clear blue sky beyond.

Then came dull and distant thudding sounds.

Retreating hoofbeats from beyond the rise told him the sniper was making off.

At once Russ Hyatt stood upright, stepped over his dead horse and advanced toward the rise, rifle stock at his cheek. Again he swung his aim in a short slow arc, ready to shoot at any sign of life. He moved soundlessly over the grama sod and in a moment was at the crest of the rise.

From there he could see a dozen miles to cedared hills heading Horse and Pole Creeks—hills which spurred southward from the Laramie Mountains. The loping dot of a horseman, by now far out of range, sent a wave of futile anger through Russ. Futile because he was afoot and couldn't give chase; and much too far away to identify either the man or his mount. It was a horse of some darkish color and could be anything but gray. The rider himself, nearly a mile away, might be any man on the range.

Three empty rifle shells, 44-40s, lay near the rock from which he'd fired to kill. A litter of cigaret butts meant he'd waited there no short while.

Questions snapped at Russ and his wits went to grips with them. *How did he know I'd come riding by? What did he have against me? Or did he take me for somebody else?*

At the moment Russ was on his way to Cheyenne from the Y Bar on upper Horse Creek. The trail he'd followed was a horse path angling southeast to hit the Deadwood-Cheyenne stage road a few miles short of the Pole Creek station. It was the logical route for a horseman riding townward from the Y Bar.

The sniper had left bootprints but they could be anyone's boots. The prints of his horse, which had been tied to a greasewood stalk just west of the brow, could be the prints of *any* shod horse. Then the shine of sunlight on glass caught Russ's eye and he picked up an empty half-pint bottle. The label on it said "Kentucky Squire Whisky." It still had a whisky smell and the label wasn't faded by weather.

Killed it while he was waitin' for me, Russ reasoned.

For what they might be worth as evidence, he dropped the half-pint bottle and the three empty shells in his jacket pocket. Then he walked back over the rise to the trail.

His lean, sun-darkened face was grim as he knelt there to take the gear from his dead horse. "He's a lowdown bum, Tony. The kind that packs a saddle dram on his hip." Most range riders liked whisky, Russ was aware; but generally they saved their thirst till they got to a bunkhouse or bar.

Walking in riding boots wasn't easy. But there was no help for it. Moving shadows on the sod made Russ pull his hatbrim low so that he couldn't see the circling buzzards. He put his carbine back in the saddle scabbard. Then he heaved the saddle gear over his left shoulder, his right hand crossing upward to grip the horn.

It wasn't far along the trail to the stage road and there Russ put the saddle down and looked at his watch. It was nearly noon, which meant that the southbound stage was soon due to pass here. The Fred Schwartz station, on Pole Creek, was its midday eating stop.

In a little while Russ saw its dust. Out of the dust came a jingle of trace chains and the crack of a whip. A top-heavy Concord coach came wheeling this way, its four-horse team at a trot.

The driver set brakes when he saw a stranded cowboy standing by his saddle. "Whoa there! Danged if it ain't Russ Hyatt!" He pulled to a stop. "Whatsa matter, fella? Didjer bronc throw yuh?"

Russ pushed out a lower lip and forced a smile. "He got shot out from under me, Red."

Red Trumbo cocked an eye. "The heck you say! Who done it?"

"Wish I knew, Red. Is there room inside for me?" The seat beside the driver was already occupied.

"Sure. Hop in."

Russ hung his saddle gear on the baggage rack and opened the coach door. Of three passengers inside, two were an army couple and the other was a girl Russ had seen more than once in Cheyenne. The lieutenant and his wife faced forward, while the girl traveling alone was on the front seat facing backward. Her billowing, flounced skirt took up most of the seat and a shovel bonnet, tied with a ribbon under her high-collared chin, hid most of her face. It was a face to make a man look twice and Russ knew right away she was Gail Garrison of the big Garrison spread on Sweetwater. Only she spent most of her time in Cheyenne where the Garrisons kept a town house and did a lot of high-society entertaining.

The only vacant seat was beside the girl, so Russ squeezed gingerly into it. "Won't crowd you more'n a few miles," he promised her. "Only as far as Pole Creek."

She turned toward him with a smile faintly quizzical, yet with reserve in it. "You're not hurt, I hope?"

It meant she'd heard him tell Trumbo about the shot horse. And the reserve in her tone meant she knew that when a cowboy gets shot at he usually isn't blameless himself. "Only my feelings," Russ said. Blond bangs showed under the hood of her bonnet and he caught himself staring. Then something punched his knee and he shifted to make room for the lieutenant's belted saber.

"Sorry," the young officer said. "I have to wear the blasted thing, you know, in or out of a stagecoach. Wilkes is my name. And this is

Mrs. Wilkes. We're being transferred from Fort Laramie to Fort Russell."

"I'm Russ Hyatt. You're in luck, I'd say, trading Laramie for Russell." Fort D. A. Russell was at the edge of Cheyenne which was the territorial capital with both a railroad and an opera house.

"You know Miss Garrison, of course?" the army wife murmured.

"Only by sight," Russ said.

Again the girl looked at him, her blue eyes narrowing as she tried to place him. "At the D Cross?" she murmured. D Cross was her father's brand.

Russ shook his head. "No. Always in Cheyenne. Once you were at the Cheyenne Club when I dropped in with a message for my boss. Another time you were getting out of a carriage at the Opera House. Another time at a band concert out at the fort . . ." He broke off suddenly as a smile from the army wife suggested that he was exposing an amazingly accurate memory.

A lump at his ribs made him wonder what caused it. Absently his hand delved into a jacket pocket and pulled a half-pint bottle partly out. As he dropped it out of sight he was aware that Gail Garrison was still turned toward him and that she'd seen the top of the bottle. Would she think what he himself had thought of the sniper? That only a low-lived bum carries a saddle dram on the range?

"Who else was in the fight?" Lieutenant Wilkes

asked curiously. "I mean besides you and the man who shot your horse."

"No one." Russ said it shortly and a little annoyed; half at himself and half at the girl. She'd turned the back of her head to him and was gazing out at the prairie. The coach was again at a trot, making dust. A few of Dave Ullman's steers grazed close to the road, with a big Campstool brand on the left flanks. Far beyond them a band of antelope went bobbing over a rise.

"Here we are!" Red Trumbo yelled from the driver's boot. The coach rolled downhill into Pole Creek. "Everybody out fer a feed while we change hosses."

The stage lurched to a stop in front of a two-storey roadhouse and bar. Fred Schwartz himself was clanging on a dinner gong. Another coach, northbound and an exact mate for this one, came thudding across the Pole Creek bridge and stopped. "Right on time, both of you!" Schwartz said to the two drivers.

Russ stepped to the ground, then turned to help Gail Garrison out. But Wilkes was next and handed both his wife and Gail from the stage. Russ tried to fall in step with Gail as she moved toward the dining-room door. But she recognized two passengers getting out of the northbound stage and turned to them with a gay welcome. "Dickie! And Edgar! What on earth are *you* doing away out here on the prairie?"

The two young men who joined her looked like Boston or New York. Their hunting corduroys had been tailored to fit. They came bounding up to Gail and each took one of her hands. "On our way up to Teschie's place," one explained, "for the deer season. And you, Gail?"

"On my way home after a visit with the John Huntons at Bordeaux," she told them. "Come, let's go in and eat. I'm starved."

As the three disappeared into the station, Russ went to the stage and unloaded his saddle gear. Then he hunted up Schwartz. "I'm on foot, Fred, unless you can sell me a horse. What've you got on hand?"

The station had a stable and corrals. Some thirty horses were in them and Schwartz took Russ for a look. Most of them were harness stock owned by the stage company. Of the few others, none suited Russ.

"Bunch of ridin' stock comin' upcrik from Mort Post's place, long about sundown," Schwartz remembered. "Maybe one of 'em'd do yuh."

"I'll hang around for a look," Russ decided. The Post horse ranch ran the best of saddle stock.

He was freshening up in the station washroom when he heard a northbound passenger telling about Cheyenne's current news sensation. "Yep, killed 'em in cold blood, the guy did. With the butt end of an axe. Just for a measly fifty-three dollars they had on 'em. But he didn't get far with it. They nabbed him and slapped him in jail at Cheyenne."

The passenger had yesterday's Cheyenne *Leader* to prove it. The date on the paper was September 10, 1883. It was passed around the washroom and Russ saw a headline. INHUMAN BUTCHERY. "Hank Mosier crushes the skulls of two camp-mates for their pocket money...."

Russ passed through the bar to the dining room and took the only vacant chair left at a long table there. Gail Garrison and her two Eastern friends were at the far end, their chatter lost in a hum of nearer talk. Food was served family-style with Mrs. Schwartz presiding. At mid-table Red Trumbo tried to tell someone about Russ's horse being shot out from under him and ordinarily he would have been pressed for details. But just now everyone was too much interested in the more sensational Mosier story from Cheyenne.

"He'd've got clean away," the northbound driver told him, "'cept fer somebody rememberin' a leetle black dawg allers follers thishere Mosier. So they spread the word and surenuff, some woman just over the Colorady line said she'd seen a guy with a leetle black dawg afollerin'."

Russ Hyatt, absorbed in watching Gail and her two Easterners, missed most of it. It wasn't strange she'd know them. Cheyenne was full of monied New Yorkers—and there were even a few titled Britishers—who owned big Wyoming ranches and who part of the time lived a sort of boiled-shirt club life in Cheyenne. Often they brought out guests like Dickie and Edgar.

From his own end of the table Russ could see through an open door into the taproom. The bar was empty during most of the meal and Russ was almost finished when a dusty rider dismounted outside and entered for a quick one. The man had a black-stubbled chin with a shine of sweat on it and he wore a black-butted gun low on the left thigh. Left-handed, Russ thought absently, then returned his attention to the table.

In a lull Gail Garrison's voice floated to him. "How long will you be at the Duck Bar, Dickie?"

Everyone knew that the Duck Bar was Hubert Teschemacher's ranch about a hundred miles north of here. Russ wasn't interested in how long Dickie would be a deer-hunting guest there. What alerted him to a tight-wire tension was a phrase from the taproom, spoken hoarsely by the lone bar customer.

"I better take a half-pint along with me, just in case of snake bite. Make it Kentucky Squire."

Abruptly Russ Hyatt left the table and went outside. Hostlers were leading fresh four-horse teams to the waiting stages. At the hitchrack was a newly arrived saddle horse and Russ took a look at the scabbard rifle. It was a 44-40. The horse was a dappled brown with sweaty flanks. He could see that it had done some hard running within the last hour or so.

Russ spoke to a hostler who was hooking up trace chains at the Deadwood-bound stage. "Notice which direction that fella rode up from?" He nodded toward the brown horse.

"He come from upcrik," the stable hand said.

"Thanks." Russ took a stand with his back to the hitchrack, elbows resting on it, his eyes fixed narrowly on the taproom door.

Last seen, the sniper had been heading west. But once out of sight he could double back east down Pole Creek to the Schwartz station. *He knows I didn't see his face so he's not worried about running into me here.*

The man was a total stranger to Russ. Nothing made sense unless he was a hired killer working for someone else. Assuming that much, Russ let logic lead him on. No kill no pay, he reasoned. So the man doubled back to try again. Russ would have to walk or catch a ride to the nearest corral, which was Fred Schwartz's. After picking up a remount Russ would continue on to Cheyenne. To earn his fee the killer could follow along and shoot from behind the first lonely cover.

Maybe it was a wrong guess, Russ admitted. Lots of men rode with 44-40s and maybe more than one of them packed a half-pint of Kentucky Squire on the hip. Maybe but not likely.

The taproom door opened and the man with the black-stubbled chin came out. He was black nearly all over—hat, shirt, belt, gun butt, boots. The hat was high-crowned and new, pushed well back on a receding hairline. A man of medium height, stocky at the shoulders and spare at the belt. He didn't look particularly dangerous. Nor did he seem startled when he saw Russ at the rack by the sweaty-flanked brown horse.

Maybe he saw me leave the table. So he's not surprised to find me here. He's had time to get a spiel ready. Russ continued to lean against the hitchrail with his elbows hooked on it. His holster flap was open but he didn't expect a go for guns. Not right in front of the station with two stageloads of passengers at the table inside.

Russ Hyatt spoke quietly as the man came up. "Who you ridin' for, Blackie?"

The man's lips smiled but his dark, smoky eyes didn't. "Reckon you got me pegged fer somebody else, mister. Alford's my name."

"My mistake, Alford. But I'd still like to know who you're ridin' for. Mind tellin' me?"

The smoky eyes narrowed and Alford's voice took an edge. "Is this a habit of yours, mister, pokin' your nose into other folks' business?"

"It's a habit I got into late this mornin'," Russ said, "when somebody took a pot at me with these." His right hand dropped to a jacket pocket and brought out three empty 44-40 shells. He balanced them in his right palm, giving Alford time for a good long stare. "Somebody who sluffed off this," Russ added. His left hand brought an empty half-pint from his other side pocket and he balanced it in his left palm. "Same brand as that saddle dram you just bought at the bar, Blackie."

"Meaning what?" Alford shot a quick sidewise glance to see if the hostlers were watching.

"Meaning I want to know who hired you to pick me off. And what for. And how much he's paying you for the job."

For the first time the black-chinned man looked dangerous. His voice was like sandpaper. "I don't usually take talk like that." He waited a cold ten seconds before adding, "And I don't see any reason to begin now."

His draw was fast. Russ looked like a setup, standing with his hands out palms up, empty shells in one and an empty half-pint in the other. But his eyes saw Alford's left elbow crook and they telegraphed to his right boot, which came in a swift upswing to kick the gun just as it cleared the holster.

It left Alford bare-handed but with wits enough to catch Hyatt's upraised leg, tipping Russ backward and off balance. But when Alford stooped to pick up the gun Russ was on him, riding him to the ground. They rolled over there, under the hitchrail, kicking, clawing, punching. In less than a minute the faces of both men were streaked with dust and blood.

Shouts from the hostlers brought passengers tumbling out of the station. Pain racked Russ Hyatt's eye as Alford's thumb gouged there. As they rolled out from under the hitchrail their combined weight cracked the half-pint bottle. Locked in a clinch Russ caught a glimpse of Gail Garrison who'd come out with the others. A woman's voice, not Gail's, exclaimed, "How disgraceful!" To most of them it would look like a common taproom brawl.

Then Schwartz and his hostlers were pulling them apart. Russ got to his feet, breathing hard, his face raw with bruises. He met Gail's eyes and wanted to explain, but something he saw there made him draw into a shell. Her look seemed to say, "What can you expect?" It hardened Russ and left him in no mood to curry favor with her.

Besides there wasn't time. One driver yelled, "All aboard for Deadwood!" The other shouted, "All aboard for Cheyenne!"

The what-can-you-expect look was still on Gail's face as Dickie and Edgar handed her into the southbound stage, then boarded the northbound themselves.

Whips cracked and the coaches rolled away in opposite directions.

"Can you prove it?" Schwartz asked when Russ charged Alford with being this morning's sniper.

"He knows danged well he can't," Alford snapped out.

Russ grimaced. He stooped to pick up the paper label from a shattered half-pint bottle. "Reckon this is about all I got," he admitted.

"It's not enough," Schwartz said.

The man with the black-stubbled chin gave a look of mixed defiance and derision. Then he stepped into the saddle of his dappled brown horse and rode away toward Cheyenne.

2

Six hours later, at sundown, Russ took the same direction himself. He'd waited all afternoon for the saddle stock due up from the Post horse ranch. The wait had been worthwhile for this blocky blue roan had a nice gait and promised both speed and endurance. "We'll be in town before midnight, Blue." That is, if they didn't get waylaid by Blackie Alford. Russ thought of the dead sorrel back on the Y Bar trail. What happened once could happen again. "We'll keep our eyes peeled, Blue Boy."

This was open prairie country, slightly rolling, and except for an occasional gully there was no likely spot for an ambush. All afternoon, resting back at the Schwartz station, Russ had raked his brain for a motive. He had no personal enemies. He wasn't due to testify in a court case. For the past two weeks he'd been breaking horses for the Y Bar but there'd been no trouble with anyone. His last regular job had been with the Boxed M, up Mesa Mountain way. At the end of the spring roundup, early in July, the entire Boxed M crew had been laid off. But there was no ill feeling about it as far as Russ knew.

Dusk came to the prairie and then starlit darkness. It lessened the hazard of an ambush. Light was now too dim for shooting except at face-to-face range. And even if Alford lurked in a gully he'd hardly be able to tell Russ from any other passing horseman.

Another hour of jogging and Russ saw the shapes of two windmills by the road. And a dark building. That would be the Nine-Mile stage station run by the Seeleys. Not an eating stop; just a watering station.

Its people had gone to bed and Russ rode on by. A little way beyond he caught up with a horseman who rode too tall and thin in the saddle to be Blackie Alford. Drawing alongside, Russ recognized an old crony and relaxed. The man was Skeets Carson of the TOT.

"Where you headin', Skeets?"

"Home," Skeets said, meaning the Oelrichs' place on Crow Creek just above Cheyenne. He borrowed makings and the two cowboys rode on at a walk, Carson looping a long skinny leg around his saddle horn. "They called me in from the roundup. Seems the boss has got a lot of people comin' out and he needs me to wrangle for 'em. What *you* been doin', Russ?"

"Gettin' shot at, Skeets." Russ told about the sniper and the run-in at the Pole Creek station.

Skeets brooded over it. "Must've took yuh for someone else. Somebody about your build who rides a sorrel."

"Could be," Russ admitted.

"Ain't seen yuh since the spring tally," Skeets

said. The TOT and the Boxed M and in fact all ranches in the county were in District Number One, as designated by the Wyoming Stockgrowers' Association. So Skeets and Russ had ridden in the same roundup, along with several hundred other riders. "What's this I hear about you gettin' laid off, Russ?"

"The whole Boxed M crew got laid off, soon as the tally was over."

"Been back over there lately?"

"Nope. Been breaking broncs for the Y Bar."

"Boxed M's got a new crew," Skeets said. His eyes squinted thoughtfully. "Kinda funny Wally Grimes'd lay one crew off, then right away go hire himself another."

Russ shrugged. He'd heard a lot of guesses and bunkhouse rumours about that one. One was that Grimes had done it as an economy measure, then changed his mind. Another was that he'd taken on an Arizona partner who wanted to bring a crew with him. "It's *his* outfit, Skeets. Reckon he can hire and fire anybody he wants."

"What's takin you to town, Russ?"

"Remember that dude I guided on an elk hunt in the Big Horns fall before last? Fella named Miles Cortney from Boston."

"I heard you talk about him once. You said he's an okay gent."

"They don't come any better, Skeets. He went back East and I didn't think I'd ever see him again. But yesterday I got a note at the Y Bar. It was from Miles Cortney. He's at the Inter-Ocean Hotel in Cheyenne and wants to see me right away."

"Another elk hunt, maybe?"

"He didn't say."

They spurred to a jog and presently saw lights off to the right. They were lights at Fort Russell about three miles northwest of Cheyenne. Russ started to look at his watch but didn't need to. From the distant post came the clear notes of a bugle blowing Taps.

A trail forked off in that direction and Skeets Carson took it. "Here's my turn-off, Russ." A short cut to the TOT would take him right past the fort barracks.

Russ Hyatt kept straight on and was soon riding down a dusty street in the northern suburbs of Cheyenne. Imposing two- and three-storey residences flanked it, some with grilled iron balconies and front-yard fountains. Most of the Wyoming cattle kings kept family homes here at the capital. People like the Garrisons and the Swans and the Careys and the Warrens and many others whose stock ran on a thousand Wyoming hills. Per capita the richest city in the world, men called Cheyenne.

And the wickedest, others said. A big New York daily, in a recent article reprinted in the Cheyenne *Leader*, had called it just that.

Russ struck Eddy Street and turned south there. This highly respectable part of town was lighted only by the stars. It was still five blocks to Sixteenth where Saloon Row would be ablaze and roaring.

But now a nearer sound came to Russ. A low rumble of voices with a sinister tone. He'd just crossed Twentieth when a mob of men appeared a block south at the corner of Nineteenth and Eddy. More than a hundred of them and at once Russ sensed what was up. He remembered the news sensation which the stagecoach had brought to the Schwartz station.

"That-there telegraph pole'll do."

"Toss yer rope over it, Bert."

"Let's get it done and go to bed."

"Quitcher snivelin', Mosier, and start sayin' yer prayers."

The struggling man didn't have a chance. The end of a rope sailed upward and caught the cross arm of a telegraph pole. The crowd swelled and blocked Eddy Street, making it impossible for Russ to pass. All he could do was sit his saddle and look on.

Then he heard another voice shouting protests, demanding that the mob disperse. For a minute the rumble quieted as the hangmen listened with a sort of cynical respect. The man who protested wasn't Sheriff Seth Sharpless. Russ failed to see Sharpless anywhere. The speaker was hatless, half-dressed in pants, shirt and suspenders—a big bald man of forty. He was Joseph Carey, mayor of Cheyenne, president of the Stockgrowers' National Bank, a power in the WSGA and owner of the CY cattle brand over in Albany and Carbon counties. "For shame!" Carey shouted. "Are you mad? Here you are only a short block from the courthouse! Almost in the very shadow of the Territorial Capitol! I say you can't do it. Take that wretch back to the jail and let the law deal with him. Disperse and go home . . ."

Impatient voices broke in on him. "Go home yourself, Joe Carey!" "The law's too daiggone slow, Joe." "Listen, Joe Carey, whenever you wanta run fer governor we'll vote fer yuh. Meantime git to hell outa here and let nature take its course."

Mayor Carey stood helpless. Fenced off by the milling crowd he couldn't even get near Mosier. The mob pulled the rope and yanked Mosier high off the ground. They let him kick half a minute, then lowered him to the street. But again they pulled the rope and raised him high overhead.

A sickness came to Russ Hyatt's stomach as he sat his horse half a block north. He couldn't get through them. So he wheeled and rode back to Twentieth to turn west there and detour the block. Looking back he again saw a black, kicking shape above the heads of the crowd. "It's fer keeps this time! Leave him swing!"

Russ turned south again at Thornes Street, rode past Henry Haas' smithy and stopped at the IXL barn at the corner of Sixteenth. The night man stalled his roan and stored his carbine in a locker. Then Russ headed afoot down Saloon Row. For two blocks every other door was a bar, all open for trade but uncommonly hushed just now. Only the more timid customers were still here, the bold and the boisterous having joined the mob. As Russ passed Duke Turpin's place the voice of the night barman came out through the hinged half-doors. "Serves the guy right. A guy'll think twice, after this, before he goes around bashin' in skulls with an axe."

The next place east was dark, quiet—the somber brick front of the First National Bank. Then another saloon and then the unlighted hulk of the Warren Block with Esselborn's more exclusive bar cornering it. From across the street a gaudy, flushed woman called to Russ through an open upper window of the Leighton House, "Is it over?" The stupid, half-frightened smile on her face revolted Russ and he didn't answer. The whole town knew, or would soon know, about the lynching of Mosier.

Another block east took Russ to Cheyenne's leading hotel, the Inter-Ocean. It was a three-storey brick with tall, arched windows. He went in and was crossing the broad lobby toward the desk when an exceptionally striking young woman stopped him. "Is it over?" she asked with a note of dread in her voice. Her words echoed those he'd just heard from a woman as different from this one as dark from day. But he knew both had the same meaning. This girl had breeding and a vivid, intelligent face under brilliant black hair and eyes.

"I'm afraid so," Russ said soberly.

She looked down at his holstered gun. "You were there?" she asked accusingly.

"Only by accident," he explained quickly. "I was ridin' down Eddy and they were blockin' the street."

Again her expression changed and her smile had a quirk of apology. "I'm glad you weren't in it. It's beastly, barbaric! Why didn't the sheriff stop it?"

"He wasn't there. The mayor tried to. But he didn't have any luck."

"Please don't think I'm rude or forward. I can't find out these things unless I ask questions. I'm Jean Markle of the New York *Globe-Sun*." With another faint smile she sat down at a lobby table, took out a notebook and began writing.

Moving on to the registry desk, Russ remembered something he'd read in the Cheyenne *Leader*. A piece signed Jean Markle and reprinted from a big New York daily. It seemed that the paper had sent a feature writer out here to report on Wyoming's fourteen-years' experience with women's suffrage. And since the subject dealt with women they'd chosen a brilliant young woman to cover it. Jean Markle. Wyoming women had been allowed to vote ever since the territory was cut off from Dakota in 1869. Had any good come of it? Had Wyoming women used their votes to refine society? Jean Markle's job was to find out.

All this Russ knew from reading the *Leader* at the Y Bar bunkhouse—for the local paper had breezily reprinted the New York *Globe-Sun* articles—a series Jean Markle was calling "The Shame of Cheyenne."

"The richest—and the wickedest—city in the world!" she'd written. "Thirty saloons and forty vice houses!" "Thirty-seven hangings in Cheyenne's short history, and only two of them legal! Women of Wyoming, what have you been doing these fourteen years?"

She could make it thirty-eight now, Russ thought grimly, with still only two of them legal!

The clerk pushed a book to him and he registered. Then his eye caught a name just over his own. George Alford, Cheyenne.

Was it Blackie? "The guy just ahead of me. When did he check in?"

"Along about sundown," the clerk said.

"Maybe he's not the same Alford I know. Is this fella stocky through the shoulders wearin' a black shirt and belt? Needs a shave, usually."

"That's the man. If he's a friend of yours you'll find him in room 25."

"Thanks. What about a Mr. Cortney from Boston?"

"You mean Mr. Miles Cortney. Yes, he's been here a week. Room 36. But tonight he's not using it. He has a guest card at the Cheyenne Club and is spending the night there."

"Much obliged." Russ was given room 29 and he went up to it. Tomorrow would be soon enough to look up Cortney and find out what he wanted. A big game hunt, more than likely. Russ opened number 29's windows. They looked out on Sixteenth. The rattle of a switch engine came to him from the Union Pacific yards, just beyond Fifteenth. Russ took off his shirt and scrubbed away the range dust. Already he'd forgotten about the Mosier affair and about the crusading young woman from New York.

For the unexplained mystery of Alford was in the foreground again. Alford who'd shot to kill from ambush, and whose room was only four doors down the hall. According to the clerk the man was in there right now. Probably in bed and asleep. If so the transom over the door would be dark.

Russ stepped into the hall for a look. He counted four doors from his own and saw a glow at the transom. It was door number 25. Alford had done a lot of hard riding today. Why would he be up at midnight? Was he alone?

Russ went into his own room and took off his boots. He belted on his holster gun, then moved quietly down the hall to number 25. Listening there he caught a faint hum of talk. It was subdued, furtive talk. Two men spoke only in whispers. Russ put his ear to the door. But it was a solid-oak door and he caught only a detached word here and there. Most of all he wanted to know who was holding this midnight powwow with Alford. If Alford had been hired to kill, he could be explaining why he'd failed. He could be getting fresh instructions.

The room was Alford's. So the other man should be leaving in a little while. This carpeted hallway was lighted by bracketed oil lamps spaced along its walls. When the visitor left, he'd have to pass Russ's door on his way to the stairs.

So Russ went back to his room, darkened it, left the door part-way open. He sat quietly on the bed, watching. Alford's departing visitor could easily be seen as he passed along the lighted hall.

Ten or more minutes dragged by. Russ listened for the click of a latch down the hall. Surely the man wouldn't stay much longer.

The first sound Russ heard was someone hurrying up the stairs from the lobby. The oncomer turned this way and passed the half-open door with quick strides. Russ glimpsed a tall slim man in cowboy hat and boots, belted and gun-slung. The face was iron-red from the sun, high-cheekboned and wide at the chin—a face strange to Russ. The man headed straight down the hall toward room 25.

Russ heard him knock there. He moved in stocking feet to his own door and peered out. The man was thumping his knuckles on door 25. Alford's sandpaper voice came from inside. "Who is it?"

"It's Judnick. Open up."

A key turned and the door opened. Russ saw Judnick step inside. The door closed and its lock clicked.

Russ slipped soundlessly down the hall to listen. This time he caught words and phrases, some of them explosive. The men in there, after hearing news brought by Judnick, for a moment were too excited to keep their voices down.

"He's right here at the hotel!" Judnick insisted. "As I come by the desk I seen his name in the book. Right below yourn, Alf."

Alford's rough, hoarse voice asked, "What room did they give him?"

"Twenty-nine," Judnick told them.

"You mean you let him get by you?" This in a low, harassed voice Russ couldn't identify. Yet it seemed vaguely familiar.

"Nothin' else I could do," Judnick explained.

"When he rid by me another guy was sidin' him. A TOT man they call Skeets."

There was a nervous silence, then the voices lowered warily to whispers. More and more Russ felt sure that the unidentified man was giving orders, and that only the luck of meeting Skeets Carson had saved his own life. Apparently Alford had arrived around sundown to report failure; after which a second killer had been sent out to waylay Hyatt.

But why? And who was paying for it?

The lighted transom suggested a way to find out. Russ slipped back to his own room, picked up a chair, carried it to the door of room 25. They might open the door and catch him here, so before mounting the chair Russ drew his forty-five gun.

Standing on the chair brought his eyes level with the transom. He pressed his face against the glass and peered in. It was a tall door which made him look downward at a steep angle. Alford was sitting on the bed, fully dressed except that his gunbelt hung from a bedpost. He'd shaved the stubble from his chin and changed his shirt. Standing in the center of the room was the lantern-jawed Judnick, hat tipped back as he licked a newly rolled cigaret. His slyly narrowed eyes were on someone sitting so close to the near wall that Hyatt, spying obliquely through the transom, could see only his knees and boots.

They were cowman's boots, not spurred, new and shiny and expensive. One of the man's hands reached out to flick the ash from a cigar and Russ's angle of sight gave him a glimpse of it. A pudgy hand, not browned by the sun. "They's no way fer you to get outa here," Judnick warned him, "without passin' right by his door. It was open as I come by. Open and dark."

Another long, nervous silence. Then Judnick went to a window to stare speculatively down at the Sixteenth Street sidewalk. He shook his head. "Too long a drop, boss. You'd break a laig."

As he turned from the window his eyes picked up Russ Hyatt's face pressed against the transom glass. In the tick of a watch he drew and fired.

The glass shattered, chips of it spiking into Russ's chin and cheek. A bullet skimmed his scalp and the shock toppled him from the chair. He hit the hall floor with every light in his brain out.

3

The sound of the shot brought people from a dozen rooms. As many more rushed up from the lobby. They found what seemed to be a dead cowboy in the hall just outside room 25. Above the door was a bullet-smashed transom.

In the open doorway stood Judnick and Alford. Judnick admitted firing the shot. "We seen a face at the transom," he explained. "The guy had a gun and he was aimin' it at George Alford. He had it jammed agin the glass and was about to blow daylight through George. So I cut loose and dropped him. That's his gun layin' right there by him."

John Chase, the hotel's two-hundred-and-fifty-pound proprietor, stooped over Hyatt and found a shallow, bloody groove down the scalp. And a bump where his head had hit the floor. "He'll live to stir up worse trouble than this," Chase said. "Somebody help me tote him to bed and call a doctor."

"He belongs in room twenty-nine," the night clerk said.

Russ was carried to his room and put on the bed. Alford and Judnick followed along, luring the crowd with them. No one thought of searching number 25 for a third man. Which made it easy for a man with spurless boots and pudgy white hands to slip out and mingle with the crowd. Anyone seeing him would take him for just one more curious guest who'd popped out at the sound of a shot.

A deputy sheriff appeared and listened to Judnick's story. Alford backed it up and the unconscious Hyatt wasn't heard at all.

"He was standing on a chair all right," the deputy concluded, "because the chair's still there and it belongs to his own room. He had his gun out because it was layin' right there by him." He turned to Alford. "What was he gunnin' you for, mister?"

"He jumped me at the Pole Crik stage station," Alford explained. "Ask anybody out there. Tried to beat hell outa me but Fred Schwartz broke it up. Then he swore he'd foller me to town and gun me."

"What was he sore about?"

"Claims someone shot his horse a few miles the other side of Pole Crik and he thought I done it. I wasn't anywhere near the place and can prove it."

"Okay," the deputy said. "If you want to swear out a charge against him I'll lock him up."

After exchanging glances with Alford, Judnick shook his head. "You can leave him go, far as I'm concerned," Alford decided. "He got a slug bounced off him, so maybe he'll know better next time."

"What about you, Chase? It's your deadfall that got shot up."

"If he'll pay for that transom glass," the hotel man said, "I won't make any charge against him. Publicizin' a gunplay wouldn't help my trade any."

The deputy seemed relieved. "Hell's to pay up at the courthouse," he said with a wry grin, "account of that Mosier lynchin'. I'd just as soon not pile any more grief on top of it. Here comes Doc. Everybody else clear out."

By the time Russ was fully conscious his head wound had been treated and bandaged. Only John Chase and the doctor were in the room with him. "It's not even skin deep," the doctor said. "What knocked him out was bumping his head on the floor. Just keep him quiet for a while." He picked up his bag and left them.

Anvils rang in Hyatt's brain but he felt better after Chase held a flask to his lips. "Where did they go?" Russ asked weakly.

"Where did who go?"

"Those three men in room twenty-five."

"Only two were in there," Chase said. Then, at Hyatt's searching look, he repeated the story told by Judnick.

"He lied by the clock," Russ said. "All I did

was peek in to see who was there. A third man was smokin' a cigar but I couldn't see his face."

A patronizing smile rode the hotel man's broad, florid face as he stood up. "I guess that rap on the head's got you kinda mixed up. Better get yourself some sleep, young fella."

When he was gone Russ got up and locked the door. He lay down again with his head thumping. How could he sleep? They'd tried to get him twice and they'd try again. That might be why they hadn't sworn out a complaint. If he was in jail they wouldn't be able to get at him. But here in a dark room, or on the street, or on the range, they could. In some way they'd get at him and next time they wouldn't miss.

Russ sat up and pulled on his boots. *They know I'm here. I'm in no shape for a fight. Not tonight anyway. So I better duck out quick.*

He went to a window and looked out. Across Sixteenth, leaning against a saloon wall, stood two men with their hats pulled low. Judnick and Alford! They were gazing obliquely upward toward this window.

Russ drew the blind and finished dressing. The mirror showed his taped head and brought a sallow grin to his lips. Not even skin deep, the doctor said. Sticking plaster held the dressing in place and when he slapped his hat on it couldn't be seen.

He sat down and wrote a note.

Dear Mr. Cortney:

Had a little trouble on the way in. You can find me at Clem Harwood's place. It's a log house right across from the east gate of the fairgrounds. Yours,

                        RUSS HYATT.

He buckled on his gunbelt, put out the light and looked warily into the hall. It was empty. Russ slipped along it to the stairs where he went up instead of down. On the third floor he found room 36 and pushed the note under its door. Miles Cortney, after his night at the Cheyenne Club, would find it when he came back to the hotel.

Rear stairs let Russ down to a dark alley. He followed it west and came out on Ferguson Street between the Delta Club and the Cheyenne Savings Bank. A driver dozed on the box of his two-horse hack, waiting for some late-homing gambler to come out of the Delta. Russ shook him awake and got in. "East gate of the fairgrounds," he said.

The hackman's mouth hung open. "You gone loco, mister? That's way out on the prairie. Ain't nobody lives out that way but Clem Harwood, and he's haulin' freight to Fort Fetterman."

The Harwood cabin was dark when they drew up there. But the latchstring was out. Russ paid the hackman and went in. "Any time you need a bunk use one of mine," Clem had told him once. They were friends since the winter of '81 when Russ, with no riding job in sight, had hired out as a teamster with one of Clem's hauling outfits.

In his young days Harwood had been a mountain man, and the habit of sleeping far away from street sounds was still strong on him. That was why he'd built this cabin blocks beyond the next most outlying house in Cheyenne.

Russ lighted a lamp and fired the stove, put on coffee and opened a can of tomatoes. Thought of Judnick and Alford made him chuckle. They were like coyotes watching an empty bird's nest. Maybe they'd break into room 29, before morning, to do a nice quiet job on him. Or maybe they'd lay for him when he went to breakfast. Russ smiled as he blew out the lamp and turned in. They'd hardly think of looking for him here, far from the settled part of town.

It was nearly noon when the voice of Miles Cortney awakened him. "Hello there. What happened to your head?"

Russ sat up, blinking. One hand reached out to take Cortney's and the other felt ruefully of a taped dressing along his scalp. "I didn't get bucked off a bronc," he grinned. "Where'd you get that hat?"

Cortney, tailor-made and as spruce as though he'd just stepped out of a bandbox, had nevertheless made one concession to Western fashion. He'd bought himself a cowman's hat, high-crowned and fawn-colored, as expensive a piece of headgear as could be found in Harrington's haberdashery in the Carey Block. He was consciously proud of it, judging by the angle it was cocked on his auburn-haired head.

"I didn't hear a hack drive up. How'd you get here, Mr. Cortney?"

"I walked. Felt like stretching my legs. And don't call me *Mr.* Cortney. Makes me feel like I don't belong out here. Call me Cort and then give me some free advice."

Russ washed the sleep out of his eyes and heated coffee. He poured two steaming cups. "Advice about what?"

The Boston man pushed the cowman's hat to the back of his head and grinned. "I'm about to buy myself a herd of cattle."

Russ wasn't much surprised. When out here hunting fall before last this man had been strongly attracted to Wyoming. He'd talked about making an investment out here someday. Many other young Easterners of like means had already made extensive livestock investments in Wyoming. Russ could name a score of them—men like the Sturgis brothers and Harry Oelrichs. Ivy League graduates who'd transplanted themselves to grama sod. Some had made good and some hadn't. All of them had found adventure and a new life.

"Cattle are zooming," Russ said. "Watch out you don't go broke. Have you picked out a buy yet?"

Cortney cupped hands over a pipe, nodding. "Yes. The Boxed M brand. But I'd like to check with you first, Russ. I'm told you kept the tally book for the Boxed M at the spring roundup."

"That's right. You mean you're buying out Wally Grimes?"

"Any reason I shouldn't? The banks say he runs high-grade native stock."

"His stuff's as good as any," Russ agreed. "What's he askin' a head?"

Cortney consulted a notebook. "Twenty-one dollars for yearlings; thirty dollars for two-year-olds; thirty dollars for mature cows and thirteen dollars for calves. I checked with John Clay who just bought a big herd from Sturgis and Goodell. He paid exactly those prices and the banks tell me Clay's the smartest cattle buyer in Wyoming."

Russ nodded. He'd read about Clay's buy in the *Leader*. "Yeh, he paid exactly those prices to stock his Quarter Circle 71 on Sweetwater. It's a boom year for cattle and you can't get good natives for less. But . . ."

"But what?"

"The quality of the Grimes stuff is good and the

price per head is right. But you've got to be sure it's all there. Don't put too much trust in a book tally."

The man from Boston laughed. "I've been warned about that. Book tallies are a standing joke at the Cheyenne Club."

"The joke started," Russ explained, "in Luke Murrin's saloon one cold winter day. Bunch of cattlemen were in there during a blizzard, worryin' about how many steers'd die in the drifts. Luke drooped an eyelid their way and said, 'Cheer up, boys; the books won't freeze.' Meanin' that some brand owners just let the fall book tally stand all winter and sell out next spring on that basis, no matter how many head froze or got stolen over winter."

Cortney was still smiling. "I'm told a number of big deals have gone through on sheer book counts."

"You heard right, Cort. Lots of million-dollar corporations have been floated in New York, London, Edinburgh, all on a book tally basis. Not a hoof ever really counted in the flesh. Someday somebody'll go broke. But in the meantime every one of those companies is payin' dividends."

"About the Wallace Grimes herd," Cortney said. "Today's September twelfth. The spring roundup wasn't over till July fifth. You kept the tally book yourself. Right?"

"That's right. I signed my name to the Boxed M

tally. Then I got Dunc Grant and Charley Fisher to initial it."

"That was just two months ago, Russ. Losses should be slight in good summer weather—and more than offset by new calves."

Russ caught the drift. "You mean you figure to buy the Boxed M brand on the basis of the spring roundup count, which we know was good as late as early July?"

"Yes. Providing you identify the signature to the tally book as the one you made yourself; and the initials you had Grant and Fisher put under your name. The banks tell me Grant and Fisher are reliable."

"As honest as daylight," Russ agreed.

"I looked up the minutes of the May meeting of the Wyoming Stockgrowers' Association. It divided Wyoming into nineteen roundup districts and set up routes and limits and foremen for each district roundup. Boxed M runs in District Number One; which takes in everything between Colorado and Fort Laramie, and everything between Nebraska and the Laramie Mountains. Its foremen were Duncan Grant and Charles Fisher."

Russ refilled the coffee cups and brooded over it. Buying a herd in the spring on a tally made the previous fall could easily bankrupt the buyer. But buying in early September on a July tally shouldn't be too risky. Russ's hand went up to scratch his head and touched the dressing over a wound there. With a jolt it reminded him of yesterday's snipings. "Hold on!" he exclaimed. "Did you tell Grimes about sending a note to me at the Y Bar?"

"Naturally. Why shouldn't I? Your name was signed to the totals. You're an old friend I can trust. So I told Grimes I'd check with you before closing the deal."

A light of understanding broke on Hyatt's face. "Don't go through with it," he warned. "It's a steal. He padded that tally some way and didn't dare let us get together. Listen." In terse words Russ told about yesterday and last night.

"And now that I think of it," he finished grimly, "Wally Grimes smokes cigars and has pudgy white hands. Betcha a saddle to a cinch ring he was the third man in Alford's room last night."

For a moment Cortney was shocked speechless. Then—"You mean he'd have you murdered in cold blood? I can't believe it! He gave me the First National Bank as a reference. He's a member of the WSGA in good standing. He has the run of the Cheyenne Club and . . ."

"Wait a minute," Russ broke in. "Have you got the tally book with you?"

The Boston man nodded and brought the Boxed M tally book from his pocket. "I insisted on showing it to you. Is this your signature?"

He spread the book open at the last page, the

one showing totals for the spring roundup. At the bottom Russ saw his own name and below this the initials of the district foremen, Duncan Grant and Charles Fisher.

To Russ's surprise there was no forgery. The signature was his own. He was sure the DG and CF were just as genuine.

When he admitted this, relief broke on Cortney's face. "So you were wrong, Russ. Your getting shot at yesterday had nothing to do with it."

Age totals were listed above the signatures and Russ studied them.

Yearling steers	2628
Yearling heifers	2340
2-yr-old steers	4681
2-yr-old heifers	4562
Mature cows	2206
Calves	1303

"That's about how many calves we branded," Russ conceded. "The figure for cows is about right too. I remember figurin' we had a fifty-nine percent calf crop."

The cow-and-calf counts were naturally impressed on Russ more clearly than any others. Primarily a spring roundup is called the calf roundup and other counts are more or less incidental, since beef is rarely shipped till late fall.

As tallyman Russ had scored in a book every time a Boxed M calf was dragged to a fire. And of course Boxed M was only one of many brands taking part in District One's roundup.

"The yearling figures look right too," Russ said. "But not the two-year-old counts. How much did you say he's chargin' you for two-year stuff?"

Cortney brought a memo from his pocket. "These are the complete sale figures, Russ."

2628 yearling steers @ $21.00	$55188.00
2340 yearling heifers @ $21.00	49140.00
4681 2-yr-old steers @ $30.00	140430.00
4562 2-yr-old heifers @ $30.00	136860.00
2206 mature cows @ $30.00	66180.00
1303 calves @ $13.00	16939.00
17720	$464737.00

The amount involved brought a low whistle from Russ. Yet he knew that in recent months many deals much larger than this one had been transacted in Cheyenne. Fat dividends and sky-rocketing beef prices throughout 1881 and 1882 had made 1883 a year of wild and blind speculation, Eastern and British investors flocking in to buy on book tally any herd offered.

John Coad, whose stuff ranged on the Platte below Fort Laramie, had just sold out to an English syndicate for $800,000.00. The Pratt and

Burt herds had changed hands for $400,000.00. Voorhees and Post had just sold their brands to a corporation for half a million. The Bosler brand of 45,000 head had brought twice that much, sight unseen. Russ thought of many others, the gigantic Swan corporation just floated in Edinburgh topping them all.

He knew too that the promoters were generally honest. They both bought and sold by book count. Sellers treated buyers as they were willing to be treated themselves. As a rule their only sin was an unrealistic optimism which blandly ignored blizzards and thieves and normal range losses. They sat snugly by the hearth of the Cheyenne Club, cheating themselves as often as they cheated anyone else—a cheerful, gallant band of armchair cattlemen who bought and sold by the book.

"They never pad a tally book," Russ muttered, thinking aloud. "Which is where Wally Grimes has gone them one better. Wally crossed two 'ones' and made 'fours' out of them. Then in the total he flagged a 'one' and made it a 'seven.' Look."

On another paper Russ rewrote the sale memo, changing only three figures. The number of yearlings, mature cows and calves remained the same. "But the 4681 2-yr-old steers should be 1681; and the 4562 2-yr-old heifers should be 1562. If you add it up that way, the total comes to 11,720 instead of 17,720. And the total price comes to $284,737.00."

Cortney stared at the figures. "But how would he dare? Too many people knew!"

"The Boxed M roundup reps knew," Russ agreed. "So he laid off the whole bunch of us soon as the spring gather was over. The cattle are scattered over a hundred miles of range so the new crew he hired won't know how many are there until after the fall roundup, which won't be over for a month yet. As for the banks here in town, and the club crowd you've been hobnobbin' with, they're so much in the habit of believin' tally books that they'd take this one in stride. You didn't ask a bank to finance the deal for you?"

Cortney shook his head. He had half a million idle in a Boston bank and had planned to pay spot cash.

"So no one had a personal interest except you! Dunc Grant and Charley Fisher might think that total looked funny, if you'd asked them. But you didn't ask them. Anyway Boxed M was only one of thirty outfits in that roundup. Thirty sets of tally figures are too many for Dunc and Charley to remember. And right now they're a long way from Cheyenne. So are all the old Boxed M men except me."

A sheepish smile formed on Cortney's face. "If you're right, Grimes was about to sell me six thousand two-year-olds which don't exist."

"For thirty a head, Cort. A cold steal of a hundred and eighty thousand. So he didn't dare let us get together...."

"You're right, Hyatt. I didn't dare let you get together." The statement came in a sad, dry tone from Wallace Grimes. Russ twisted toward the open door and saw Grimes standing there with his pale, plump palms upspread and with a what-else-can-I-do look on his face. At his elbows stood Judnick and Alford, each with an aimed gun.

4

Hyatt's gunbelt hung on a nail, out of his reach. There'd been no reason to belt it on this morning. He felt trapped, helpless to protect either himself or Cortney.

Alford and Judnick came in, gun hammers cocked, and the look on Alford's face made Russ brace for bullet shock. Grimes himself looked scared enough to be dangerous. Leaving Russ alive meant prison for Grimes. The WSGA itself would see to that. It couldn't afford to let one of its members pad a tally book to cheat an investor of a hundred and eighty thousand dollars. A scandal like that could crash the market and frighten livestock investors everywhere. The entire Wyoming boom could burst like a pricked bubble.

"How did you find me?" Russ asked them.

"We follered this-here dude," Judnick explained slyly.

Mainly Russ watched Grimes' pale, fleshy face as the man closed the door. Panic streaked it. The man's stubby pink tongue licked his lower lip and shadows swam in his eyes. "You don't leave us any choice, Cortney. If there was another way out we'd take it. There's just nothing we can do except . . ."

Alford broke in impatiently. "Then what are we waiting for? Let's be done with it and get outa here."

All it needed was a nod of Grimes' head to unleash the triggers of both gunmen. So Russ began talking fast. "Think it over," he warned. "Suppose we're found dead here! Who will they suspect? First off, the law'll find out you had a deal on with Miles Cortney. Then they'll find out Cort sent for me and I had a horse shot out from under me on the way in. The whole thing'll be on the front page and somebody'll remember a face in the hotel hallway last night. Your face, Wally Grimes, as you slipped out of room twenty-five and sneaked through the crowd."

By the flicker of Grimes' eyes Russ knew that every one of those considerations had occurred to him. "And on the way in," Russ followed up, "I met Skeets Carson of the Oelrichs outfit. Told him Miles Cortney sent for me."

"Search him, Alford," Grimes said.

With a gun at Hyatt's ribs Alford went through pockets and found the note sent by Cortney to the Y Bar. Reading it brought a slight relief to Grimes. "He sent for you—but it doesn't say why. Once you guided him on an elk hunt. People will think he wanted you to do it again."

"Van!" The single shrill syllable came from Cortney. He was facing the cabin's west window. Before he could cry out again Judnick's gun

barrel came down hard on his head and crumpled him to the floor.

And Russ, looking through the same window, saw what had drawn his friend's outcry. The nearest neighbor was two blocks away but directly across the way lay the town's ten-acre fairgrounds. In the middle of it was a bandstand and circling it ran a quarter-mile race track.

Two riders were cantering around the track and had just reached the end nearest to this cabin. One was a girl on a sidesaddle, her long skirt swinging almost to the ground. The man with her was a bare-headed blond—a social favorite here in Cheyenne and a member of one of the leading cattle families. The deserted fairgrounds track made a convenient bridle path for a couple out for a morning ride.

Russ felt the bore of a gun at his head and heard Alford warn, "Sing soft, cowboy!"

The man and the girl, a bare stone's throw away, had reined up and were gazing curiously toward the cabin. Apparently they'd heard Cortney's outcry and were puzzled. Russ, half a mind to risk everything by yelling himself, suddenly recognized the girl's face. She was the one he'd met on yesterday's stage—Gail Garrison.

"They come over here," Judnick warned, "they'll be in the same boat you are."

It was true. Glen Van Tassen, out for a morning ride with a girl, wouldn't be armed. He'd be no help in a fight. And these men would as soon kill four witnesses as two.

The fact gagged Russ. Presently he saw the pair canter on around the track. They made several complete circuits of it and then took off south along Dodge Street. Six blocks would take them to the Cheyenne Club and maybe they'd stop for cool drinks there.

The closeness of the call rubbed the rawness of Grimes' worry and brought him to a decision. "You do it here," he warned his men, "and somebody might hear the shots."

"I can get a buckboard," Alford offered. "Then we can haul 'em out on the range somewhere."

"And nobody'll ever see us again," Russ filled in. "Where will that leave you, Grimes? A Boston millionaire comes out here to dicker with you for a herd of cattle and suddenly he disappears into thin air. Same thing happens to a cowboy he sent for. So here comes the sheriff to ask you questions, Grimes. Better take my advice and think this through to the end."

Grimes took out a cigar and trimmed it nervously. This whole thing was too big for him, Russ thought. He wasn't nearly big enough mentally, or bold enough, to handle a deal like this.

On the floor Cortney groaned and sat up, holding his head. As he got to his feet Judnick gave him a shove which sent him reeling to a bunk. Then Judnick turned snappishly to Grimes. "Well, make up your mind."

"I don't like taking them away in daylight." Again Grimes' tongue circled his lips. "We better wait till dark."

"And what then?" Russ prodded. "Don't keep us in suspense, Grimes. You drive away with us after dark, us all neatly covered with a tarp . . . and what then?"

"We'll leave it to Lou." Grimes looked at Judnick with his nerve-shot face twisting. "You and Alf sit on them while I go talk to Lou."

Judnick gave a sour nod. "We got plenty time," he admitted, "if we're gonna be stuck here till dark anyway."

A decision to pass the buck to a person named Lou chased some of the harassed lines from Grimes' face. He hurried out, heading south down Dodge.

And a question in Hyatt's mind was now answered. The bigness and boldness of this fraud hadn't fit Wally Grimes. Grimes was a coward with a small-bore mind. Now it seemed there was a man higher up—someone who pulled strings from a safe distance.

"Who's Lou?" Russ asked curiously.

Alford's grin mocked him. "What you don't know won't skin your neck, cowboy."

Russ raked his mind for the name Lou. It could be the beginning of either a first name or a last name. It could be the name of a man or a woman. Did Grimes have a wife? Or some underworld charmer from west of Eddy Street with wits shrewder than his own? Or was it some man in the upper world who kept under cover? Chances were that it was no mere thug gunny like Alford or Judnick but someone of standing who gave orders even to Grimes himself.

It was late afternoon when Grimes came back. Relief on his broad, moist face told Russ that "Lou" had offered some plausible way out.

"I should've thought of it myself," Grimes said to Alford and Judnick. "Here's what we do. We don't need to knock off these johnnies. Murder never pays dividends, Lou says. We just take 'em to a hideout and keep 'em there a month or so and then turn 'em loose. But first we lay a plant that they've gone on a hunt, like they did before."

"You're loco!" Judnick exploded. "If we turn 'em loose, they'll squeal their heads off."

"Let them," Grimes said. He lighted a cigar and puffed it calmly. "By then we'll be a long way off. What you don't know, Jud, is that Cortney's not the only man in town with a big checkbook and tryin' to buy in on the cattle boom. Lou knows two or three more just like him. So we sell out to one of them fast. Then we cut for Mexico or Peru. Think a minute. That's where we'd have to go anyway, even if the Cortney deal had gone through. Fall roundup tallies'll give us away come November, no matter who we sell out to."

Russ searched for a flaw in it. Grimes would have to run far and fast if he worked the scheme on anyone at all. Another dupe would set the law on him, regardless of whether Cortney was released or murdered. But there was still something loose and unexplained about it. The risks for Grimes were too big unless he was under some hard pressure. The fraud wouldn't be clear, Russ thought, until he found out where and why and how "Lou" came into it.

"Danged if I like it," Judnick griped. "Means somebody'll be tied up sittin' on these jiggers at the hideout. Coupla months, maybe. Simpler to let 'em have it right now."

"What burns me up," Alford complained, "is that everybody's gotta run except Lou. Lou can grab a cut and stay right here in Cheyenne." Alford took a half-pint from his hip and upended it. He passed it to Judnick but Grimes waved it away.

Who, Russ kept wondering, was Lou? Man or woman? Surely he or she had something on Grimes and could call every turn Grimes made. Cheyenne was full of adventurers and adventuresses. Schemers and gamblers, some in silks and some in boiled shirts. Nothing made sense unless one of them held a whip over Grimes and was using him as a cat's-paw in a swindle. A swindle which would make a fugitive of Grimes and still leave Lou entrenched and unsuspected in Cheyenne.

Miles Cortney spoke wearily from the bunk. "You overlook something, Grimes. I've a roomful of baggage at the hotel. I owe a bill there."

"Same goes for me," Russ put in, "at the IXL barn. I got a horse in a stall and a rifle in a locker. Nobody'll believe I went off on a hunt leavin' my bronc and rifle in town."

Grimes smiled. "Lou thought of that. So we'll plug it up." He laid paper and pencil on the table. "Cortney, you write a note to the hotel. Tell 'em to give bearer your baggage. Bearer will pay your bill. Hyatt, you write one to the IXL barn."

"And if we don't?" Russ bickered.

Grimes shrugged. "You got two choices, Lou says. You know what the other one is."

"Yeh," Alford's sandpaper voice cut in. "Do like we say or eat your last supper right now. Bullets with black-powder sauce."

Cortney came to the table. "How do we know," he asked, "that you'll turn us loose after the getaway?"

Grimes mopped his face and spoke coaxingly. "Because it makes sense for us to turn you loose. We'd gain nothing by gunning you—long as we keep you from spoiling the deal with someone else."

The Boston man looked dubiously at Russ.

"What do you think? Are they lying, or bluffing, or what?

"They're not bluffing." Of that much Russ was sure. "They'll crack down if we don't do what they say. Not that I'd trust 'em any further than I could throw a steer by the tail."

"All I want's an out," Grimes coaxed. He fixed a sallow smile on Cortney. "This way it works out smooth for everybody. Tomorrow, at the banks or at the club, people'll ask how my deal with you is coming along. I'll say it fell through and you've gone off hunting to the high country. Who with? they'll ask. Same guide you had before, I'll say. So they won't expect you back for weeks. When you *do* come back, with a story about being held in a hideout, I'll be a long way from Wyoming."

Ten to one the man was lying, Russ thought. Yet accepting the terms would at least gain time. Better to risk murder at the end of a long trail than to touch off sure and sudden murder right now.

So Russ shrugged, thrust out a lip and nodded. Cortney picked up the pencil and began a note to the hotel.

"You be the bearer, Alford," Grimes said. "First you go to the Bon Ton livery for the buckboard and trail kit we keep there. Next you drive to the Inter-Ocean to pick up Cortney's baggage. Then stop at the IXL for Hyatt's outfit. Tie the horse to the endgate and get here with it an hour after sundown."

Cortney finished his note. And Russ, hating himself for it, wrote a short one to the IXL barnman.

Alford collected both notes and then helped himself to Cortney's wallet. "After I pay the bills," he promised impudently, "I'll bring you the change."

His eyelid drooped in a wink meant for Judnick. A cracked laugh came from Grimes. Russ looked from face to face and knew that murder was still on the cards. They'd simply made murder safer by preparing a plausible reason for the disappearance of the victims.

"We've been taken, Cort," Russ said bitterly. He heard a wagon creak along Twenty-second Street, only a block south. It might be his last chance. With a wagoneer within earshot these gunnies might hesitate to shoot. Right now Alford, with a cat-in-the-cream grin on his face, was stuffing the two notes and the wallet into his pocket.

So Russ dived head-on at his middle. As he dived he yelled like a Comanche, hoping Miles Cortney would do the same. His head banged into Alford and the man fell hard on his back with Russ on top, yelling, clawing, punching. Maybe the wagoneer would hear and come, or give an alarm . . .

A shout from Cortney was choked off almost before it started as Judnick for the second time batted him down with a gun. Russ, grappling with Alford, didn't see it. Nor the shiny, spurless boot of Wally Grimes as it aimed a kick at his head. Alford lay inert under him, winded and punch-drunk. Then kicks from the sharp-toed boot of Grimes began thumping on Hyatt's skull.

Judnick's hand snatched his collar and jerked him to his feet. Russ saw bloodshot eyes over the iron-red, high-boned face—that and a poised knife. The throbs in his brain were like hammers on an anvil and his knees were water, folding under him. He saw the knife go back to strike.

"Hold it, Jud!" The husky warning came from Grimes. "You'll mess the place up. Wait till you get 'em out in the woods."

Russ no longer could hear the creak of wheels on Twenty-second. Had the wagoneer reined up to listen?

Judnick shifted the knife to his left hand and punched with his right. It was a chin punch and Hyatt went reeling. He didn't know when he hit the cabin floor.

5

The buckboard had been jolting him a long time before Russ was fully conscious of it. Numbing pain cut at his wrists and ankles and fire burned in his head. Cloth wadded into his mouth stifled his groan. Gradually he knew it was night time and he was in the bed of a moving wagon.

A tarp was spread over him and as he squirmed his elbow touched another man. He knew then that Cortney lay beside him and they were being driven over prairie sod. The ruts of a road would make smoother going than this. By keeping off the roads they wouldn't meet other wagons.

The last words of Grimes reechoed in Hyatt's brain. "Wait till you get 'em out in the woods."

That would mean a long ride. There were no woods anywhere close to Cheyenne. Barring an occasional cottonwood or willow along the water courses, this was a treeless prairie. The nearest real forest would be high in the Laramie Mountains some seventy miles northwest of Cheyenne. There were patches of scrub cedar much nearer, toward the heads of Pole and Horse Creeks, but you didn't think of them as woods. "Wait till you get 'em out in the woods!" *That's where we're being hauled now.* Out to the woods where dead men tell no tales, even when their bones are finally found there.

Russ squirmed under the tarp and got a corner of it free from his face. He looked up at a cloudy, starless sky. His feet pointed forward and his head was at the endgate. Two men sat on the buckboard seat and another rode a little way ahead, on horseback, leading two saddled mounts. In the dimness Russ saw them only as shapes. One of the led horses could be his own blue roan. The shorter man on the wagon seat was probably Grimes. The driver took a half-pint from his hip and drank from it. That made him Alford and the man asaddle must be Judnick.

The cords at his wrists and ankles were unbreakable and Russ soon quit squirming. His hands were tied in front of him and he could move them in short arcs, the heels of his palms always touching. The gag didn't bother him long. After spitting it out he rolled to his side and groped with his bound hands for the face of Miles Cortney. He knew Cortney was still alive by the warmth of his lips. His fingers gouged a wadded rag from Cortney's mouth. "Quiet!" The creak of wheels covered his whisper.

Then Russ lay on his back for a while, trying to locate himself. Stars were hidden. They were bumping over virgin sod in an unknown direction, blackness walling them on every side.

Then again, as a night ago, Russ heard a faraway bugle. This time it blew Call to Quarters and came from his left, which meant he was moving northwest. The time was half an hour before Taps and Fort Russell lay to the southwest. So this rig was cutting across the prairie to hit Pole Creek somewhere well above the Schwartz stage station.

Were they bound for the Boxed M? Boxed M headquarters were near the head of Pole Creek on a rugged tableland called Mesa Mountain, spurring off of Pole Mountain, which in turn spurred off the Laramies. Some of the crew there would be away at the fall roundup. Those left at the Boxed M, if any, could be toughies like Judnick and Alford. A drive to the Boxed M would take all night.

Alford whipped up his team. "Get along there." A trotting gait nearly jolted the breath from Russ.

"Bear a bit to the left," Judnick called back. He was riding ahead to pick the best route. Russ saw him twist in the saddle. "How they ridin'?"

"Like sheep in a boxcar," Alford said.

A match scratched as Grimes lighted a cigar. Then for a mile or so Russ heard only the creak of wheels. When Grimes spoke his voice was relaxed. "I'm glad we got by the fort. Not likely to run into anyone from here on. Tomorrow I'll take the buckboard back to town and the rest of you can go on by saddle."

"Lota trouble for nothing!" Alford complained. "Right here'd be as good a place as any. We could dump 'em in the first gully and be done."

"Lou's plan's a lot safer," Grimes argued. "That way everything gets explained pat and no questions asked."

"Let's have it again," Alford growled.

"You take 'em to the high country and set up camp. It has to be a place where any smart guide would take a dude for elk or mountain sheep. You put up a tent. You scatter their duffel around. You make lots of fire ashes and leave tin cans like they've been there a week. You shoot a deer and leave it hanging there half skinned."

"Then we plug 'em," Alford finished. "And make off with their stock and saddles and money and rifles. It's outlaw country. If anyone ever finds 'em, it was outlaws done it. Outlaws stumble on a rich dude and his guide, so they take 'em. Sheriff books it that way and the case is closed."

Talk stopped and the buckboard bumped on. Russ lay quiet in the wagon bed, barely breathing, wondering if Cortney had heard them outline Lou's blueprint for murder.

"Slow up," Judnick said from a length ahead. "Here's where we drop into bottomland."

There was a grind of brakes as the wagon took a down-sloping bluff. Then they were on level ground again, this time on smooth, grassy meadow. "Pole Creek Valley," Russ whispered to Cortney.

A string of ranches lay along Pole Creek but

Alford wouldn't pass within shouting distance of a house. The rig had turned due west, hugging the south bluff. The settlements were close to the creek which ran generally along the valley's north edge.

A hound howled in the distance. That would be the Warner place, Russ decided. He knew Pole Creek like the back of his hand. Les Warner kept a pack of hounds.

No use shouting. The house was too far away. The Warners would be asleep, this late. Peering to the north Russ saw no lighted window.

The hound howled again and the buckboard rolled on, Alford trotting his team whenever he had smooth going. He slowed to cross a gully, then whipped to a trot again.

A few miles further on Russ heard metallic, scraping sounds alternating with blunt bumps. The Spicer ranch, he concluded, because along upper Pole Creek only the Spicers had a windmill. Again he peered across the bottomland and saw no light.

Half an hour beyond the windmill he heard a braying mule. That could be the Flagg ranch, or maybe Otto Stump's place. Both Flagg and Stump owned mule teams.

If it was the Stump place they were more than a dozen miles upcreek from the stage road—and heading in the general direction of the Boxed M on Mesa Mountain. A cloud broke briefly to show a thin moon. By its position in the sky Russ figured it was an hour or two after midnight.

Then, from not far up-valley, came the bellow of a bull. A cow mooed and was answered by the bawl of her calf. Other cattle sounds came from ahead, a scattering of sounds reaching from bluff to bluff of the valley. Alford swore and stopped his team. "Is that a campfire I see upcrik?"

"Looks like it," Judnick said. "Coupla punchers on night herd, maybe. Looks like two-three hundred head bedded down right in front of us."

"We better not drive through them," Grimes advised. So Alford reined to the left and soon the rig was crunching upgrade over gravel. Russ knew they were deserting the Pole Creek bottom to detour a bunch of night-herded cattle. Alford swore softly. "We'll lose an hour by this!"

The night herders, Russ reasoned, belonged to the fall roundup whose main camp right now would be thirty miles north of here on Bear Creek. Occasionally a roundup's main drive by-passed some crack in the hills and cattle there were later gathered by clean-up men. Such a bunch could be pushed on to join the main roundup, moving only by day. At night the bunch would bed down, the herders keeping an on-circle man asaddle to make sure the cattle didn't scatter.

They'd challenge Alford if he disturbed or drove through the cattle. So he was giving them a wide berth. It forced him out of the valley and put him on rough, side-hill going. For here a grama sod prairie no longer bordered the valley. Rocks and pebbles crunched under wheels and Russ could smell cedar. He remembered a hillside cedar brake a few miles southwest of the Stump place. "You're makin' a hell of a racket," Judnick said.

"How can I help it?" Alford snapped back. "Ever time I hit a rock it starts rollin'. Can't see ten feet ahead. I better stop till you pick out a way to go."

The buckboard stopped. Gravel crackled under hooves as Judnick rode ahead to scout a route.

In a little while his voice came from the dark. "This way, Alf. Bear a bit uphill and take it slow. Won't be more'n a mile of it. Then we can drop back into the bottom."

The rig crunched on, rocks sliding as the wheels dislodged them. The cedar smell grew stronger. Something brushed across Hyatt's face like a pungent-smelling broom.

It was the bough of a cedar tree. In the dark Alford had driven too close to it. "Watch where you're going!" Grimes complained. He too had been slapped by the bough.

Decision came to Russ. He held his bound hands upward and waited. Waited and prayed to be slapped again by the springy, needled limb of a cedar.

If it happened, the fingers of his wrist-bound

hands must grasp it. And never let go! Judnick was scouting ahead. Alford was straining his eyes to pick a route. Russ set his teeth and waited. His bruised body ached like sin and his strength was at a low ebb. But this was a *must*. He *must* get out of the wagon and there was only one way.

Slap! A bough brushed his upturned face and he snatched, missing. The wagon crunched on. "Watch where you're going!" Grimes grumbled again.

Cedars were on every side and Alford couldn't miss them all. Again a bough brushed Russ and his fingers clutched it with grim desperation. There was a jerk—and he felt himself slipping headfirst over the endgate. The crackling of wheels on gravel smothered all other sound.

Darkness made a curtain as Russ held his grip. So long as he held it, and the wagon kept moving, one of two things must happen. Either the bough would break or the wagon would roll out from under him.

The bough didn't break.

6

By holding on till the last second Russ made his legs hit the ground before his head. Strength oozed out of him and he lay face down on the hillside gravel, trembling like a spent kitten.

The buckboard didn't stop. As the wheel sounds got further away Russ raised to his hands and knees, footbound and wristbound, and began an awkward crawl. They'd soon miss him and come back. They'd beat about for him in the dark. So he wriggled away in a random direction and when crawling seemed too slow he rolled. He rolled downslope like a barrel, bumped into a cedar, veered off from it, wriggling, crawling, rolling in the dark.

His breath came in gasps as he stopped to listen. The wheel sounds had almost faded. Again he crawled and rolled alternately, and again bumped into a cedar. This time it was a low-skirted cedar with its bottom branches sweeping the ground.

From far in the night came a yell. "He's gone! We must've bumped him out!"

A shrillness from Wally Grimes split the dark. "What are we waiting for? Go back and pick him up!"

The wheel sounds began again, reversing direction. They grew louder and nearer.

Russ crouched against the ground-sweeping skirts of a cedar. Hiding was his best chance. So he crawled under the cedar boughs to the trunk, the outspread, down-slanting foliage screening him like a tent. In the dark they'd have trouble finding him. But daylight would be a different story. Russ lay on his back, arrows of pain shooting through him, and tried to guess how long till morning. Light was his enemy, darkness his only friend.

Wheel, hoof and voice sounds came closer. He caught words from Judnick. "Where the hell are we? I can't even find our track."

"We should've brought a lantern. Strike a match, Jud."

Through the curtain of cedar needles Russ saw a tiny flicker. It was barely forty yards up-slope.

Alford was on hands and knees looking for sign. The harassed voice of Grimes reached Russ. "He can't get far all tied up like that. Spread out and look for him."

They moved apart and Russ heard them groping. Other matches flickered. One was held to a cigar and Russ knew the man was Grimes. "He can't get far," Grimes kept assuring them. "We didn't bump him out in the meadow. I looked back and saw him right about here."

The cigar came nearer to Russ while the other searchers moved farther away. The pink glow passed barely six steps to the right of Russ. Up the hillside Judnick called to Alford. "Better get back to your rig, Alf. First thing you know we'll lose the dude too."

Gravel crunched as Alford moved to the buckboard. Then came his voice. "He's still on ice. I'll tie him to the seat and make sure."

There was more circling and groping and calling back and forth. After a while the searchers met not more than twenty yards from Russ. "Damn this blindman's bluff!" Judnick growled. "Give me daylight and I could find him in ten minutes."

"I don't like hangin' around here too long," Alford fretted. "Come daylight they might see us from that camp. What if they took a ride over here for a howdy! Us with the dude all trussed up in the wagon."

Grimes puffed nervously on his cigar, weighing the chances. "All right," he decided. "You drive on with Cortney. Jud and I'll stay here with the saddle horses. Soon as we find Hyatt we'll catch up with you."

"Suppose you don't find him!"

"We're sheriff bait, if he gets away from us."

Again Grimes puffed his cigar. "If Hyatt gets away," he concluded, "we've got to switch plans. In that case we'll need Cortney for a hostage."

"Whatta yuh mean, hostage?"

"A hostage," Grimes explained, "is a hole card. An ace in the hole. If Hyatt gets away we've got to keep him from talking. We've still got Cortney, I can tell him. Long as he keeps his mouth shut we let Cortney stay alive. But the minute he makes trouble, in or out of court, it's good-bye Cortney."

"It won't come to that," Judnick said. "We'll find him in the next hour or so and ketch up with you, Alf. Get going."

Russ heard wheel sounds as Alford drove the buckboard on westerly toward Pole Mountain. It left Grimes and Judnick standing near the low-skirted cedar. "We better begin at the tire tracks," Judnick advised. "Then you go one way and I'll go the other."

Grimes tossed away his cigar and followed Judnick to the three saddle horses. There they stopped, talked in low tones, struck a few matches. Judnick moved slowly one way and Grimes the other, Judnick leading two horses and Grimes one.

A pink glow just beyond his screen of boughs caught Russ's eye. The glow wouldn't last long. Another minute and the cigar would be dead. The thought sent Russ wriggling out from under his shelter. His bound hands scooped up the half-smoked cigar. The glow was dimming. He put the cigar between his lips and puffed it red again.

Keeping it there he held his wrists to the glow and let fire eat at a cord. The cord was a moosehide boot lace and didn't burn readily. Hot ash stung Russ's wrist like a hornet. All the while he kept puffing to keep the cigar alive.

The cord snapped and his hands moved gratefully apart. Then he dropped the cigar to fumble furiously at the knot binding his ankles. His fingers were stiff, numbed, like pegs reaching from his swollen wrists. They couldn't take hold on the knot down there.

So he snatched the cigar, puffed it till the end was again red, held it to the ankle cord. He held it there through a sweating minute. Would the thing never burn through? Was the cigar going out? He couldn't puff it and hold it to his ankles at the same time. From the dark he heard boot and hoof crunch gravel and the sounds drew nearer. "Find anything, Jud?" Grimes was leading his horse this way.

Judnick didn't answer. And Russ saw with dismay that the redness was gone from his torch. The ash had gone cold on him. Despair settled over Russ as he scrambled awkwardly to his bound feet. His hands were free but when he tried to run the ankle cord tripped him. He plunged headlong down a slope, sliding on his chest and face.

Squirming, crawling, he slithered on down the hill. From uphill came the voice of Grimes. "I hear him, Jud. Come running."

A dry stick snapped under Russ. His fingers closed on the biggest end of it. There was nothing left except that his hands were free and he could at least swing one swipe in the dark.

He scrambled upright, ankles pinioned, his right hand clubbing the stick. He could hear Grimes but couldn't see him. Russ hopped a few steps to the deeper, darker shadow of a cedar—and strangely the hops didn't trip him. Elation shocked him as he realized the ankle cord had snapped. He'd burned part way through it and his last few kicks had completed the break.

"Where are you, Grimes?" It was Judnick yelling from uphill.

"This way, Jud. I heard him just a little piece below me."

"Hang on to your horse," Judnick warned. "If he gets his hands on it we'll lose him."

Russ could hear Judnick's stumbling run in this direction. They'd be on him in a minute. One peep of moonlight through the clouds and they'd see him. He had no gun or strength to fight them, so Russ turned and ran down the hill. He was nearer to the toe of it than he knew for in a minute he was on level, bottomland sod. It could be a Pole Creek meadow only a few miles above the Stump place.

Over it Russ ran blindly, heading toward cattle sounds to the northeast. For even when cattle bed down for the night there are always a few restless ones in a bunch of three hundred. Most of them would be lying down, asleep or contentedly chewing cuds. But from a few came movement and sound—an occasional low bellow or bawl.

Such sounds made a guide for Russ Hyatt as he raced toward them, through inky dark, as weak as a newborn calf yet forcing himself on and on. Here on meadow sod he crunched no gravel. Back of him he heard the thuds of two horsemen. Grimes and Judnick, who'd been leading horses, were now mounted. Judnick's shout reached him, "Head him off before he makes that camp!" Fury rattled his voice and Russ hoped he'd start shooting. In the dark he'd hit nothing and the shots might carry to a night herder.

A low dark shape in Russ's path was a bedded steer. As he came plunging at it from the dark the beast got up, hind legs first, then forelegs, and made off with a bawl of alarm. Beyond was a calf curled in sleep and Russ all but tripped over it. The calf's mother called frantically from close by.

Almost at once the entire herd was up, at first only restless and mildly disturbed. Then the chorus of lowing sharpened in pitch as two horsemen plunged in among the cattle. The stamping became a milling and lows became hoarse bellows of panic. Russ, afoot and in among them, kept stumbling on toward the creek. A camp of cowboys should be there, at least one of them awake and on herd duty.

Judnick yelled: "Look out! They're stampedin'! We better get to hell outa here!"

Russ tripped and went flat on his face with pounding hooves all about. Cattle thundered by and over him. Grimes and Judnick, asaddle, wouldn't be caught by the stampede. When Judnick's voice came again Russ heard a note of relief in it. "I guess this'll fix his clock, Wally. Let's ketch up with Alf."

Grimes answered him in a shaky voice. "*You* catch up with Alf, Jud. I'm heading for Cheyenne."

A cloven hoof kicked Russ in the head and he heard no more.

Russ Hyatt looked up at the polished spruce rafters of a bunkhouse. It had to be a bunkhouse because double-deck bunks lined two sides. Otherwise it was more like a clubroom. A lamp on a reading table had a yellow silk shade. There were rugs and a shelf of books. And this mattress was softer than any bunkshack tick had a right to be.

An open window let in afternoon sunlight and gay voices. Womenfolks were out there, laughing, like a party of some kind was going on. Russ tried to think of some ranch on Pole Creek where they'd have a duded-up bunkhouse. Not the Stump place, or the Spicer or Warner ranches. Not even Mort Post's horse ranch would be fancied up like this, even if Mort *did* own a bank in town.

How long had he been here? His head was clear and he didn't feel particularly sick. He put his hand to his scalp and felt the scar of a bullet groove, almost healed over. The dressing was gone from it. Then he saw a Cheyenne *Leader* on a chair by the bunk. He reached for it, looked at the date. September 16th! His tangle with Grimes was on the 12th. Had he been here four days? The last he could remember was cattle running over him.

He searched through the paper for the story. All he found was a short follow-up.

> What happened to the cowboy Hyatt is still a mystery. His injuries are healing and he takes normal nourishment, but his memory seems blocked. Doctors think the block is temporary and that he'll soon explain everything. He was overrun by stampeding cattle and picked up by night herders. He is now convalescing at the TOT on Crow Creek.

Why the TOT? Russ wondered. Half a dozen ranches were nearer to where he'd been found.

But if they'd cut straight toward Cheyenne with him, to put him in a hospital, the shortest route would take them by Harry Oelrichs' TOT, which was only seven miles up Crow Creek from Cheyenne. His friend Skeets Carson was a hand there. It would be like Skeets to make them put Russ in his own bunk while he rode for a doctor.

Where was Skeets now? Russ raised on an elbow to look out the window. A party was going on all right. The ranch yard was full of livery rigs from town. At the corrals a pitching bronco was circling the round pen with a gallery looking on. Russ saw ladies with bright parasols and a dozen or more cronies of Harry Oelrichs. The champagne crowd, he called them. Some of them owned Wyoming ranches where they never showed up except in hunting season. Sissies, some of them, playing cowboy for the thrill of it. An exception was Oelrichs himself, who played harder than any of them, yet who knew the cow business from the sod up and could show rope scars to prove it.

Russ looked across to the ranchhouse. The screened porches had wicker rockers full of guests bantering back and forth. A Chinese servant padded between the house and a cottonwood grove by the creek. Drinks were being served there, Russ thought. The bunkhouse crew would be at the corrals, roping and riding broncos.

He must find Skeets. There was something he must tell Skeets. Details of his abduction came flooding back to Hyatt's mind. Grimes! Judnick and Alford making off with Miles Cortney!

Russ bounced out of the bunk and found his boots under it. The rest of his clothes hung on pegs and he dressed hurriedly. What had they done with Cortney? He must set the law on Grimes. He must get a posse started on the trail of a buckboard, to rescue Miles Cortney.

Russ couldn't find his own hat. He picked up another at random, slapped it on and left the bunkhouse. The biggest crowd was at the corrals and he headed that way to tell them about Grimes. He'd shout Grimes' guilt from the housetops and then . . .

And then what? Russ came to a helpless stop as he remembered. Hostage was the word used by Grimes. If he told tales on Grimes, in or out of court, Cortney's life would be forfeit. Cort would be killed at some unknown hideout.

It stopped Russ cold and sealed his lips. He was gagged as long as they held Cortney. He'd sign Cort's death warrant if he told on Grimes.

Yet if he didn't, in the end they'd kill Russ himself and let the secret die with him. No doubt a bullet or a knife would have found him already except for the protection of the TOT bunkhouse. The first time he rode a lonely trail, or walked down a dark street in Cheyenne, a knife or a bullet would come.

He decided to tell one man. And one only. Skeets Carson. He'd swear Skeets to silence until Cortney was found. That way the secret of guilt would still live, even if Russ Hyatt didn't.

7

He got to the roundpen just in time to see Buck Ringo take a fall. An outlaw horse kept circling the pen, head down, trying to pitch off the empty saddle. Cheers and jeers came from the gallery. Cheers from the guests and jeers from Ringo's bunkmates. Sleek young bachelors from Cheyenne and their hoop-skirted ladies stood on benches, looking over the roundpen fence. Most of them were too absorbed to notice Russ; those who saw him perhaps took him for some livery stable roustabout who'd driven a guest from town.

Skeets wasn't in the corral crowd. So Russ went into the main barn and passed through it, coming out on the bank of Crow Creek. Voices drew him into a cottonwood grove where he found four couples sipping drinks in the cool shade.

The prettiest of the four girls was Gail Garrison and the man with her was Gerry Lorton. Russ didn't know the other three young men; but they looked like good-time boys who wouldn't know a hackamore from a surcingle. Gerry Lorton, though, in spite of his thin, blond mustache and club clothes, was a practical ranchman. He was a tall, hard-muscled man only a few years older than Russ himself, who until a year ago had operated from the saddle one of the biggest brands in the county. Just now he was too busy courting Gail Garrison to notice a trampish, disheveled cowboy staring at him through shadows of the grove.

The stare was merely curious because Russ suddenly remembered that it was the Boxed M brand which this adventurous blond bachelor had once owned and operated; and that a year ago he'd sold it to Wally Grimes. Since then Gerald Lorton had lived in Cheyenne where he brokered land and cattle stocks. Report had it that he'd made two trips to New York and one to Scotland to line up investors for new Wyoming corporations. His sale of the Boxed M to Grimes had occurred just before Hyatt's season as a rider there.

In fact, until now Russ had only seen Lorton three times. Once coming out of the Opera House with Gail Garrison; once dancing with her at the fort; and once at a rifle shoot below town. He'd never forget that rifle match last March between Major Talbot and Skew Johnson—until then called the two best shots in Wyoming. For Gerry Lorton had challenged the winner and won, with all of Cheyenne looking on.

Just now the four men were standing, their backs to Russ, while the four girls sat on a rustic bench. Glasses were held high as Lorton proposed heartily, "Here's to Tally-ho Harry!"

They drank. The plumpest of the girls giggled. And Gail said: "We're having supper at the club, aren't we? Do you suppose Harry'll drive us in?"

"Of course he will, Gail. With six-in-hand agallop all the way."

Then the plump girl looked past the men and stifled a scream. "That man! Look!"

She'd seen Russ staring from the trees. And with his five-day stubble of beard he looked like a scarecrow outlaw in flight through the bush. He smiled an apology. "Sorry. I was just huntin' for Skeets Carson. Have you folks seen him?"

As the four men turned toward him a sudden stiffening of Gerald Lorton puzzled Russ. The man's brilliant green eyes seemed oddly alert. But Russ was most of all puzzled by Gail Garrison. She got up and came to him with concern and sympathy.

"It's our patient," she explained to the others. "Didn't they tell you? They brought him in from Pole Creek and he's supposed to be in bed." She looked at Russ and added anxiously, "Are you all right?"

"I feel fine." The girl's impulsive sympathy both puzzled and embarrassed Russ. "I was just looking for Skeets . . ."

"But you shouldn't be wandering around, after what happened!"

"What *did* happen?" one of the men asked curiously. And another said: "When they picked you up you had a boot-lace cord tied around each wrist and ankle. Who the devil did it?"

Under Gail's blue-eyed gaze Russ was on the point of blurting out the truth. But some strange tension in the air stopped him. And an odd note in the voice of Gerald Lorton as the man said, "I don't suppose you remember, do you, Hyatt?"

Was it a warning? Was it a veiled threat? Or did Russ only imagine it? Of the eight people facing Russ, seven struck him as normally mystified and sympathetic. The exception was Lorton. Something in the man's green-eyed gaze made Russ wonder; his careless question reared up like a wall meant to shut off any other answer than the one Lorton gave himself.

Russ met his eyes—steady, steel-green eyes under golden brows and a bronzed forehead— and tried to read a thought or purpose. Lorton who a year ago had sold the Boxed M to Wally Grimes! Was there a connection?

The momentary sense of tension gave Russ pause long enough to let him think of Miles Cortney. His first duty was to Cortney. If he told the truth it would all be in tomorrow's *Leader*. And somewhere in a distant hideout Cort would pay with his life.

So Russ drooped his lips. He shrugged and shook his head. "Afraid I can't," he said. "Somebody batted me down in the dark. Next I knew a stampede was trompin' over me."

Lorton seemed to relax. The man brought out a pipe and stoked it. Russ's sense of crisis melted away. But Gail Garrison looked at him with a doubt in her clear blue eyes. Like she guessed he was holding something back. Then she turned to the others and said lightly: "Don't keep him on his feet answering questions. Can't you see he ought to be in bed? Gerry, you go find his friend Skeets. Send Skeets to the bunkhouse." She smiled at Russ. "That's where I'm taking you right now. Come."

She took his arm and her concern for him drove all thought of Lorton from Russ's mind. He was walking on air as she led him out of the grove and walked him toward the bunkhouse. She was firm about it, like a nurse who overtakes a wandering patient. The mystery of her absorbed and charmed Russ during that brief march across the ranch yard. Why the change in this girl? At the Schwartz stage station she'd treated him like a brawling saddle bum—the kind who rode with a dram on his hip and began fighting at the drop of a hat.

She'd been cool and even rude to him that day. Maybe she knew it and was trying to make up for it. They were almost to the bunkhouse steps when she gave him the clew.

"I feel guilty," she admitted. "I mean, as though it's all my fault."

Nothing could have amazed him more. *"Your*

fault? How can it be your fault if a bunch of cattle runs over me!"

They stopped at the steps. "Sit down, won't you," Gail said almost shyly, "while we wait for Skeets."

She sat on the steps of the TOT bunkhouse. When Russ sat beside her she looked at him with an odd smile. "You know a freighter named Clem Harwood, don't you? He keeps a cabin right across from the fairgrounds."

Russ braced himself. How much did she know? Cautiously he said, "Sure I know Clem Harwood. Why?"

"A few days ago a friend and I went horseback riding around the fairgrounds track. We thought we heard a cry for help from Harwood's cabin. We weren't sure. But we should have gone over there to see about it. If we had, the cattle wouldn't have run over you early the next morning, in a Pole Creek meadow."

She'd scored a bull's-eye. Yet how could she know? Again Russ Hyatt's impulse was to tell her the truth, and all of it. But again he remembered Miles Cortney. "You thought it was *me* yelling from the cabin?"

"Not then," she said. "But two days later an item in the *Leader* mentioned Clem Harwood's return from a freighting trip. Somebody raided his cabin, Harwood said, and took the laces out of a pair of boots. Nothing else was missing. The boots themselves hadn't been carried off. Just a pair of moosehide boot laces. But the cabin showed signs of a scuffle and that's why he was suspicious."

"Well?"

Her level gaze searched Russ. "The men who found you," she said, "say you had a piece of moosehide boot lace around each wrist and ankle."

"So you jumped to the conclusion," Russ filled in with an uneasy laugh, "that I was the fella in the cabin who yelled for help?"

"Weren't you?"

"Nope, I wasn't," Russ told her promptly. And technically it was the truth. The man whose cry she'd heard was Cortney, not himself. "So you've been blamin' yourself for nothing. Here comes Skeets."

Gerald Lorton came up with Skeets Carson. "What's going on?" Skeets demanded. "Who let you outa bed, cowboy?"

Gail stood up. "You'll see he goes back there at once, won't you, Skeets?"

"Don't fret yourself about him," Skeets grinned. "He ain't worth it. Besides he's too tough to kill. What's your hurry, folks?" he added as Gail took Lorton's arm and started away.

"*Do* take care of yourself," Gail called back to Russ. She moved on with Lorton and joined a crowd on the house porch.

In the bunkhouse Russ got stubborn when Skeets tried to make him go to bed. "Daylight's aburnin', Skeets. There's things we gotta do. And fast."

"Such as?"

"It's just between the two of us," Russ cautioned.

"I'm a clam," Skeets said. "Start giving."

Russ sat on a bunk and rolled a cigaret. "Make sure we're alone, Skeets."

"Everybody's at the corral," Skeets said, "wranglin' broncs and dudes. You mean you know who tied you up?"

Russ nodded. "Wally Grimes. And a couple of hired men named Judnick and Alford."

Skeets whistled softly. Then he brought out brandy and poured two drinks. "I figgered it could be Judnick and Alford," he admitted. "Seein' as Alford had a run-in with you on the road and Judnick took a pop at you through a transom, like I heard in town. But Wally Grimes!" Again the TOT rider whistled his surprise. "He's a topflight brand owner, Grimes is. He's strictly Cheyenne Club, WSGA and First National Bank! Why would he hogtie you and haul you to Pole Crik?"

"Listen and make up your own mind, Skeets." As quickly as possible Russ gave out the full story.

"A book tally deal, huh?" Skeets marveled. "Great jumpin' Jupiter! Book tallies are in style,

I understand, providin' you don't boost figures in the book. And this tally's boosted, you say, by six thousand head! And all done apurpose with fraud aforethought! If it ever comes out, the WSGA'll skin Grimes alive."

"And jail him for life," Russ agreed. "Which is why he had to put Cort and me on ice. Right now he's lining up another investor to take Cort's place. Claims if I give him time to make the deal and run, Cort'll be turned loose. Can we believe him?"

Skeets snorted. "Not on a stack of Bibles!"

"Just the same," Russ brooded, "I'm gagged as long as they've got Cort. You're the only one who knows. I need your help, Skeets."

"You've got it, pardner." Skeets took a hitch at his gunbelt and his eyes flashed. "When and where do I start shootin'?"

"You'll have to get a layoff from the TOT," Russ reminded him. "No tellin' how long this'll take us."

"Sure," Skeets agreed. "Just deal the cards and I'll play 'em."

"First, fix me up with a horse and guns. Alf and Jud took mine. Then I'll lope into Cheyenne and have a talk with Grimes."

"And me?"

"You ride to the cedar hillside where I dropped off the buckboard. Pick up wheel tracks and follow 'em. If they go to the Boxed M, say you're out huntin' stray horses and stay all night there. Size the outfit up."

"Will do," Skeets promised.

"What do you know about this new Boxed M crew Grimes took on after the spring tally?"

"Most of them are out on the fall gather," Skeets said. "I met 'em up there and they're mostly Colorado boys. All but one who's from Arizony. Guy named Shorty Goss. Funny thing is the Boxed M foreman didn't join the roundup 'cept for a coupla days. Then he went back to the ranch."

"What's this foreman's name?"

"Name of Spoffard. Hails from Kansas."

"Did he say so?"

"He didn't need to. Plenty of people've heard about Spot Spoffard. Made a name for himself as a town-tamin' marshal back in the seventies. Abilene, or Dodge, or some other of those hell-raisin' railheads. They say Spoffard buried fourteen gun-fannin' Texans in eight months, after shootin' it out with 'em on Main Street. He got so good at it they had to fire him and ever since then he's been punchin' cows."

"In Wyoming?"

"Not till he signed on with Grimes. His last stop before that was Arizony, they say."

Russ smiled dryly. "Glad it was Alford they sent to get me 'stead of Spoffard." He shot an oblique glance at Skeets and asked abruptly,

"What do you know about Gerald Lorton?"

The apparent irrelevance puzzled Skeets. "Lorton? Not much. 'Cept he's the best rifle shot in Wyoming. Every time there's a party out here he always brings Gail Garrison."

"He sold his ranch about a year ago. Remember?"

Skeets shrugged. "He'll have him another one someday, I bet, and just about the biggest one in Wyoming. Leastwise that's what everybody says."

His friend's meaning was clear enough and it depressed Russ. Until five days ago he'd scarcely given a thought to Gail Garrison. As sole heiress of the big D Cross spread on Sweetwater, she'd someday make the man of her choice a power among the cattle kings of the territory. The path of her life was far removed from forty-dollar cowboys like Russ Hyatt. Yet pangs of resentful jealousy pinched Russ. Skeets was no doubt right. The lucky man would be Gerry Lorton and he'd fit the part like a glove. A man who could rule the big Garrison outfit with a firm, steady hand and at the same time play Prince Charming in a box at the Opera House, at dinner at the Cheyenne Club or a masked ball at Fort Russell.

All this time, from the ranch yard, the gay chatter of guests drifted in to Russ and Skeets. Now came a clatter of wheels. Russ heard prancing horses and barking dogs—the crack of a whip and a shout from Harry Oelrichs himself. "Tally-ho! Tally-ho!"

Skeets grinned. "Happens every time he throws a party. Let's watch 'em roll."

From the bunkhouse door they saw a six-in-hand tally-ho drawn up in front of the main house. Oelrichs was on the driving seat. "Tally-ho for town!" he yelled again.

Two spotted coach hounds, sleek Dalmatians, were leaping and barking. Polished silver gleamed from the harness of six plumed and spirited horses. Men began handing ladies into the coach. "An hour from now," Skeets chuckled, "they'll be drinkin' champagne at the club."

"Where the heck did he get that rig, Skeets?"

"Imported it from London, I heard. Just to drive his guests back and forth between the ranch and town. Last party he threw who do you reckon he had out here?"

"Who?"

"Big-time actress from New York named Lily Langtry. She made a one-night stand at the Cheyenne Opera House and after the show Harry tally-hoed her out here for a midnight feed. It made her miss her train to Salt Lake and the troupe had to go on without her."

Russ nodded. The *Leader* had carried a story about it.

"Last call. Tally-ho for town!" the host shouted. The coach was full. With the whip snapping and coach dogs leaping, the coach rolled away with its six-in-hand agallop.

There hadn't been room for everyone. So the rest of the guests got into buggies and carriages to follow toward Cheyenne. The road would take them right past the Fort Russell parade grounds with a thousand soldiers cheering from the barracks.

The last rig to pull out was Gerald Lorton's. Gail Garrison sat beside him and as they passed through the gate she turned to wave a handkerchief and call back, "Make him stay in bed, Skeets." Lorton cracked his whip and the lurch of increased speed made her drop a tiny square of silk to the dust.

The rig rolled on. And Russ started walking toward the gate. "Where you goin', cowboy?" Skeets demanded.

At the gate Russ picked up a lacy, scented handkerchief. Returning it would make an excuse to see Gail again.

8

A shade paler and thinner than on his last trip to Cheyenne, Russ Hyatt dismounted at the northwest corner of Seventeenth and Ferguson to tie at a hitchrail there. The Carey Block stood on this corner with the Stockgrowers' National Bank occupying the ground floor. Through a window Russ saw President Joe Carey himself at his desk.

Above stairs were offices for lawyers, doctors and promoters. As he moved toward a stairway Russ drew curious glances. The forty-five at his hip was a sight common enough in Cheyenne; but recent news about Hyatt made him more than an ordinary mark for bar and sidewalk gossip. A Duck Bar man hailed him. "Ever figger out who done it, Russ?" And a Campstool rider sang out, "Don't let 'em sneak up on you, cowboy."

Russ went up to the Carey Block's second-floor hall. His boots thumped the board floor as he tramped along it looking at names on the doors. The door he wanted was labelled:

MESA MOUNTAIN CATTLE COMPANY

It was the business name of the Boxed M ranch. Quietly Russ opened the door, stepped inside and closed it behind him. "How's business, Wally? Lined up another sucker yet?"

A cigar fell from Wally Grimes' lips. He sat stiffly at his desk and his wide, fleshy face took a fish-belly pallor. His eyes fixed on the butt of Hyatt's gun and his soft plump hands raised a little, open, to make it clear that if Hyatt shot him down he'd be shooting an unarmed man. The fear in his eyes begged mercy of Hyatt.

"I'm not gunning you," Russ said with a cold smile. "Not right upstairs over Joe Carey's bank. Providin', that is, you haven't already gunned Cortney. What happened to him, Grimes?"

Relief leaked into the man's eyes and he began breathing again. Then he got up, went to the door and looked both ways along the hall. When it was closed again, he said with a husky slyness, "Three days after you last saw him he was doing all right."

"How do I know you're not lying?"

"I got proof." Grimes opened a desk drawer and brought out a newspaper. "You know his signature, Hyatt. If you don't, compare it with the one on this." Grimes tossed on the desk a note from Cortney which Russ had received at the Y Bar, and which had been taken from him at Clem Harwood's cabin.

"Look at the date of the newspaper," Grimes invited.

It was the September 16 issue of the Cheyenne

Leader and across its front page Miles Cortney had signed his name. The writing was definitely Cortney's, proving that the man was alive at least three days after the abduction.

"Today's the eighteenth," Russ remembered. "How do I know you didn't gun him yesterday or the day before?"

"Come back next week," Grimes promised, "and I'll show you his name on a newspaper dated today."

"You keep on provin' he's alive, do you, long as I don't call in a sheriff?"

"Not so loud," Grimes whispered. "Somebody might hear us from the hall." He cut the tip from a fresh cigar with an unsteady hand. "Put it this way, Hyatt. Nothing will happen to Cortney as long as nothing happens to me."

"Meantime," Russ said bitterly, "you've got a sniper waiting in the first gulch I happen to ride by. But don't count too much on that, Grimes. I've let one other person in on it, just in case I get sniped."

"Who?" Grimes echoed nervously.

"If I told you," Russ said with a thin smile, "you'd have *him* sniped too."

"Him?" Grimes stressed the word in a slight tone of relief. "I thought maybe . . ."

He broke off suddenly, ran his tongue around his lips, brought out a handkerchief to mop his moist, sallow face. His odd emphasis on a pronoun flashed a disturbing new angle to Russ.

"You thought it might be a woman? What woman? Did Lou tell you it might be a girl?" Russ stood by the desk and towered over Grimes. "What made you think I'd let a girl get dragged into this?"

When Grimes didn't answer, Russ slapped him hard on the mouth. "Get this. Whoever Lou is, you can tell him I'm not making bullet bait out of a woman. The one person I told is a man. You'll know who he is if I'm found dead in some gulch or alley. So will the sheriff and all Cheyenne."

Russ left him and went down to the street with the new angle churning in his brain. Why had Grimes seemed relieved at learning Russ had confided only in a man? A scene in a cottonwood grove came back to Russ. Eight of Oelrichs' guests there, among them Gail Garrison and Gerald Lorton! And his own feeling of a tension, an inflection of warning or a veiled threat from Lorton. Gail leading him off to the bunkhouse steps, waiting alone with him there for more than ten minutes! Did Grimes know about that?

If he did, only one of four men could have told him. And of the four, only Lorton had enough iron in him to be the mastermind back of Wally Grimes.

Were Lorton and "Lou" one and the same?

His wits grappling with it, Russ crossed

diagonally to the post office and stood just inside its open door. From here he could watch both stairways coming down from the Carey Block's upper floor. Grimes might rush to Lou with a report. If Lou was Lorton, he'd be relieved to know the girl he planned to marry had been given no hint of the truth. In any case Hyatt's call would need to be reported to Lou.

An emigrant's wagon drew up, its team the usual spectacle of sharp ribs and patched harness. The head of the family came into the post office while two scrawny little boys pushed up a side of the canvas to stare out at the traffic of Cheyenne. An old woman and a ragged child huddled in the wagon bed while a bony hound hunched in the feed box and shivered. A starvation outfit, Russ thought. At the same moment a spanking carriage rolled down Ferguson drawn by matched trotters, with Will Swan driving and his sister Louise beside him. While arm-in-arm along Seventeenth, fresh from a late breakfast at the club, came Tom Sturgis of the Bridlebit and Sir Moreton Frewen of the Powder River Cattle Company. They turned into the Stockgrowers' National where Sturgis was a director.

"The washed and the unwashed! Quite a contrast, isn't it, Mr. Hyatt?"

The voice came from Russ's elbow and he turned to face Jean Markle of the New York *Globe-Sun*. He remembered she'd been sent out here to find out why fourteen years of women's suffrage hadn't softened up Wyoming. Her dark brown eyes looked past Russ with a gentle sympathy at the emigrant wagon. "The half," she sighed, "that knoweth not how the other half lives!"

When he'd met her in a hotel lobby just after the Mosier lynching, he hadn't told her his name. At his questioning look she explained: "You've been in the news, Mr. Hyatt. And after all I work for a newspaper."

She was different, Russ thought. A lot different from most of those flounce-skirted butterflies he'd seen riding away in the Oelrichs' tally-ho. "Did you do a piece on the lynching?" he asked.

"I meant to." Her eyes flashed and a new firmness came to her lips. "I went to the county jail next morning to find out just how he'd been taken from his cell. But what I saw at the jail made me forget Mosier. The jail itself is the biggest story of all, far more sinister than any one lynching."

"Yeh, what's wrong with it?" Russ asked curiously. He'd never looked in at either the city or county jail.

What she told him seemed irrelevant. "Listen, Mr. Hyatt. The other evening the British members of the Cheyenne Club gave a dinner to American members who happened to be in town. Fifty-one sat down at the table. They drank ninety bottles of champagne. The new lighting system was turned on with the announcement that this was the first club in America to have electric lights. Which is true. Then the toastmaster boasted that the company present represented ownership of one hundred million dollars' worth of land and cattle. Which is also true."

"What's that got to do with the jail?" Russ puzzled.

"Take a look at it sometime and you'll see. Why, it's the most shocking scandal . . ."

"Excuse me, please. There goes the fella I'm waiting for." Russ darted out of the post office, turning south along the east sidewalk.

Wally Grimes had popped out of the Carey Block and was on the west walk heading toward Sixteenth. He must be kept in sight, so Russ stayed nearly opposite. Maybe Jean Markle would think he had bad manners, breaking away right while she was explaining something. But he couldn't risk losing Grimes.

As Grimes hurried by Nagle's grocery, his furtive glance over his shoulder made Russ dodge into the doorway of the Delta Club. The town's second most popular gambling spot, the Gold Room, was a door south of Nagle's and Grimes seemed on the point of going in there. Then he changed his mind. Russ saw him continue on and turn west on Sixteenth.

By the time Russ made that turn Grimes had passed the Warren Block and was entering the First National Bank. Alex Swan's bank, some called it. When Russ got to its plate-glass window he saw Wally Grimes cashing a check.

His hesitation at the Gold Room, Russ thought, could have been with the idea of cashing a check there. But he'd gone on around the corner to a bank. Not to be caught spying, Russ crossed to Hoyt's drugstore and waited there till Grimes came out. He saw the man move on west along Sixteenth. He crossed Eddy Street and continued on. He was looking for someone. For beyond Eddy Russ saw Grimes look into every saloon as he passed. Which was about at every other door, for here began the really tough district of Cheyenne.

Saloon Row, Jean Markle had called it in one of her *Globe-Sun* pieces. She hadn't overdrawn it any, Russ admitted as his eyes followed Grimes. Saloon after saloon with each getting more disreputable the further you went west. Range bums; tramps kicked off the U.P. trains. Sidewalks and bars were cluttered with them, with here and there a heavy-gunned outlaw with a price on his head. And just to the north, westerly from O'Neil Street, some thirty wide-open kip joints.

Wally Grimes headed into this hell's acre. Why? Russ wondered. It seemed to spoil his theory that

Lou was Gerald Lorton. Lorton belonged in the other end of town.

Russ moved on, keeping across the street and a little back of Grimes. Teams at the racks made all the screen he needed. How big, he wondered, was that check Grimes had stopped to cash?

At Barney's Bar, half a block beyond O'Neil, Grimes slipped in through latticed half-doors. Russ crossed the street to look over them himself. He saw the shaved, skull-like head of a Chinese bartender and a dozen third-rate customers. A few sat at beer tables with women from across the alley. Wally Grimes, a white-collared brand owner, would be conspicuous in a joint like this. *He's got a bee stinging him,* Russ thought, *coming here in daylight!*

He saw Grimes carry a drink to an empty table. The man who joined him there was a cut above the other customers. At least he was sober and rigged out like a range rider. He was a short man in a tall hat, booted and spurred and gun-slung. The hat slanted down and Russ saw only the lower half of a beardless, full-jawed face.

Grimes spoke to him in fast, nervous whispers. Russ was too far away to catch anything. He saw Grimes pass an envelope to the man who stowed it in an inside jacket pocket. The envelope might be a message to someone, or it could hold money just drawn from the bank.

Grimes left his drink untasted. As he came out,

Russ backed into a poolroom next door to keep from being seen. He waited till Grimes was fifty steps east before again looking into Barney's Bar. The short, tall-hatted gunman was gone—which meant he'd left by the alley door.

Russ stepped inside and spoke to a fat, sleepy man on a stool behind the cigar counter. "Guy just went out by the alley. Know who he is, Barney?"

His guess that the fat man was the dive's proprietor paid off. Maybe it flattered Barney that a clean-cut cowboy like this one should know his name. "They call him Idaho," Barney confided. "He ain't been around long. Slick hand with a pool cue, they say, and still slicker with a gun."

"Thanks." An impulse to follow Idaho tugged at Russ. But a stronger one made him go out and hurry after Grimes. From here Grimes might go straight to Lou.

Russ glimpsed Grimes a block east as the man turned north on Eddy. Breaking into a run, Russ drew curious stares. When he looked up Eddy he saw Grimes coming out of Wes Moyer's clubroom stuffing cigars in his pocket. Stopping to buy cigars meant he was no longer in a hurry. The man lighted a cigar and kept on past Dyer's Hotel. There a stockman hailed him. "How'd that deal of yours come out, Wally? The one with the fella from Boston."

"It fell through," Grimes explained. "He went off on a hunt somewhere."

Russ saw him turn east along Seventeenth and at the Carey Block go up the stairway to his office. And Russ knew he'd guessed wrong. The man was too smart to risk a daylight call on Lou.

It might be that the envelope contained a message to Lou and was being delivered by Idaho. Russ wished he'd followed Idaho instead of Grimes. It was too late now. In mid-block he turned into Luke Murrin's saloon to see what he could see and hear what he could hear.

The place wore a high polish, as usual, and was crackling with cattle talk. The most influential men of the territory did their drinking here. As a hub of inside information Colonel Luke Murrin was second only to the Cheyenne Club itself. Of the customers in sight now, at least half were WSGA members. Some of them could write a six-figure check good at the bank, buy or sell ten thousand steers by book tally, or decide between now and sundown to take their wives on a pleasure trip to New York.

Colonel Murrin himself, a florid man with a heavy gold watch chain spanning his fancy vest, stood just inside the door as Russ entered. He was a perfect host and knew everyone, even a stray cowboy like Hyatt. "Glad to see you around, Hyatt." As he shook hands heartily, his outstretched arm showed a detachable cuff with a monogrammed cuff button. "That was a raw break you had over on Pole Creek. By the way, how does it happen that Boston man—what's his name, Cortney?—didn't take you on as a guide? You guided him fall before last, as I remember."

"We missed connections this time," Russ evaded, moving on to the bar.

There he saw big Hi Kelly of the M2 on Chugwater, Frank Wolcott from Deer Creek and Luke Voorhees who operated the Deadwood stage line. A dozen other brand owners were there as Russ ordered a short beer and listened to the talk. Talk was of good times. Prices, profits, calf crops—every prospect pleased and the goose hung high. Some of these men had grown rich in Wyoming. Others had come here straight from Harvard or Oxford with fat checkbooks, and had grown still richer as the beef bonanza boomed up and on. Russ caught phrases like "We'll ship a trainload per week through November," or "Just picked up a herd from Texas," or "We're boosting our dividend this quarter."

Book count and no surrender! Russ thought. No wonder that men like Miles Cortney were swarming out here, eager to invest.

He left the place with a sense of depression. Time was racing by and he was getting nowhere. Crossing to the Carey Block hitchrail he picked up his horse. After stabling it at the IXL he walked moodily toward the Inter-Ocean Hotel.

One possibility cheered him a little. Maybe Grimes had sent Idaho on a long ride to the hideout where they were holding Cortney. The envelope could contain only the front page of today's *Leader*. By making Cortney sign the dated paper Grimes could prove his prisoner was still alive. He'd need such proof to keep Russ from going to the law.

On the way to the hotel Russ nursed that theory to squeeze whatever comfort he could from it.

It blew up as he entered the Inter-Ocean lobby. A man in a far corner was the short, tall-hatted gunman, Idaho. He was peering over the top of a newspaper and right away Russ knew why he was there. *He's waiting for me. Grimes told him I always take a room here. That money was pay in advance—for murder.*

To test it Russ didn't register for a room. He bought a sack of cigaret tobacco and walked out. He strolled south along Hill to the Union Pacific depot. There he looked back and saw Idaho. The man was idling some sixty steps behind him. *But he won't do it here,* Russ concluded. *He'll wait till dark. Till then he'll just make sure I don't leave town.*

Russ looked at the train board, as though interested in departures, then struck west along Fifteenth to Ferguson. There he went into the Railroad House and took a lobby chair. He saw Idaho loaf by on the other side of the street.

Russ pretended not to see him. He went out and walked north to Seventeenth, turned east there and walked four blocks to Dodge Street. All that way Idaho kept about a block back of him and Russ was getting downright mad about it. But there was nothing he could do except turn on the man and fight.

Maybe that was what Idaho wanted. A gunfight which he could claim was started by its victim. Russ decided not to be baited into anything like that. He kept his back to the man and here at the corner of Seventeenth and Dodge he saw the famous Cheyenne Club.

It was a big rambling brick with a mansard roof and a skylight over the main foyer—the top half-storey glass-enclosed to make an observation lounge overlooking Cheyenne. Wide porches fronted on two streets and on each was a row of rocking chairs. Cottonwoods on the Dodge Street side made shade for the east veranda, and half a dozen members were idling there. Russ climbed steps to the south porch, which was sunny and unoccupied. The door stood invitingly open and he went in. He'd been here more than once on some errand for an employer.

Usually Thomas, the pint-size assistant steward, met callers in the entrance hall and asked their pleasure. This time Thomas wasn't in sight, so Russ stepped into the main lounge wondering if he'd run into Gerald Lorton. He hadn't quite made up his mind what to say to Lorton. He might ask if Lorton knew where he could find Mr. Miles Cortney. If Lorton wasn't Lou, no harm would be done; if he *was,* his face might give him away.

The lounge was empty except for two elderly members by the hearth, absorbed in discussion of the cattle market. Russ didn't disturb them. Always the richness of this place subdued him a little. Its costly paintings, deep carpets and brocaded draperies. A click of ivory drew Russ to a doorway; he looked in and saw President Phil Dater himself at billiards with Fred De Billier of the Duck Bar. Dater waved a friendly hand as he saw the cowboy looking in. Cowboys straight from the range often dropped in here for orders. "Make yourself at home," Dater said cheerily. "Ring for Thomas if you need anything." There'd never been any snobbery here. Hospitality was rule number one at the Cheyenne Club and once under its roof, any cowpuncher was as good as a king.

Russ strolled through another doorway and found a bar with a mirrored cabinet, deserted at this late morning hour. Beyond still another door he saw a spacious dining room with a long spread of linen and silver under its glittering chandelier. Thomas was setting table for the midday meal. "May I serve you, sir?" he asked Russ. Even the servants here had absorbed some of the open-range democracy of Wyoming.

"Just wonderin' if Mr. Gerald Lorton's around anywhere."

"He's on the east veranda. I just served him a julep there. I'll go tell him you're here, sir."

"Don't bother," Russ said. "I'll find him myself. Thanks."

He recrossed the entrance hall and passed through a library. Three walls there were solid with books, and the reading tables had the latest magazines. A windburned cattleman lay asleep in an armchair with a New York paper spread open in his lap. Russ tiptoed by him to French doors which gave to the east veranda.

Six men sat in rockers there, facing the street. Each had a tall drink in hand. The leftmost was Gerald Lorton.

Their backs were to Russ as he stood in the open French doorway. A scheme to test Lorton popped into his mind. Suppose he were to speak one short, sudden word! A name! The name Lou! If only one of the six men turned his head, and that one was Lorton, it would be all the answer Russ needed.

For a moment he weighed the idea, planning the exact pitch of his voice. He mustn't call out the name explosively, or too sharply, else all six men would turn and look. A conversational tone would be right, Russ decided.

"Lou," he said quietly.

The reaction wasn't the one he expected.

Gerald Lorton did *not* turn his head. The five other men did, all of them idly curious, but not Gerald Lorton.

Lorton merely froze. He kept his face forward. All he did was stiffen—and drop his iced drink. The glass crashed on the tile of the porch floor.

" 'Scuse me, gents," Russ said. Without a word more he re-crossed the library and went out by the south door.

9

When he got to the Seventeenth Street sidewalk Idaho wasn't in sight. Yet Russ had a feeling the man was watching from somewhere. He sauntered west toward the business section and didn't look back till he'd crossed Ransome Street.

A block behind him came the short, tall-hatted gunman.

Again the man's dogged insolence brought red anger to Hyatt. In mid-block, squarely in front of the Alex Swan residence, he stopped to let Idaho catch up. Maybe some straight talk would scare the man off. Like—"What are you waiting for, Idaho? You want a gunfight, let's have it right now."

But Idaho didn't catch up. When Russ stopped, he stopped too. When Russ moved on, the killer moved on too, keeping a full block behind. All pretense was dropped. No more leaning against walls or picking flowers or gazing into windows. It was all in the open now. The followed man knew and the follower knew he knew. *He'll wait till dark, though. Right now he's just making sure I don't leave town.*

At Hill Street Russ stopped in front of the Opera House where a queue of people were buying tickets for tonight's show. According to the posters it was Fay Templeton in *La Belle Coquette*. All the boiled shirts in town would be there, with their ladies, and the thought brought Gail Garrison to mind.

More than likely she'd come with Gerald Lorton. And there wasn't a thing Russ could do to stop it.

Then he remembered her handkerchief—the one she'd dropped at the TOT gate. It was neatly folded in his breast pocket. He wanted to see her again. And why shouldn't he? The sidewalks were free and she lived only a few blocks out Hill. He could knock on her door and say he'd come to return the lost handkerchief.

So Russ started north, for the moment forgetting Idaho. At Nineteenth he passed the Congregational Church and the Garrison house was just beyond it. He came to its lawn with the spiked iron fence and the stone fountain and the cast-iron deer and the lane of lilacs. His hand was on the gatelatch when he remembered to look back.

Idaho was less than a block behind him. The man stopped, a short, gun-heavy figure under a high, peaked hat. Bleak frustration slapped at Russ as he realized he didn't dare turn in here.

If he did, Idaho would report his call on Gail to Grimes and Lou. And they wouldn't know it was just to return a piece of lace and silk. Coming right after a dropped glass on the club porch, they'd think Russ came to tell her Lorton was a swindler named Lou—the mastermind behind fraud and murder.

They'd be absolutely sure of it! Which would give them exactly the same motive to destroy Gail that they had to destroy Russ himself. They were a ruthless crew and they'd stop at nothing.

The stalemate brought a bitter fury to Russ. At the moment the only outlet for it was Idaho. Idaho who'd followed him all over town! Idaho with a gun on his hip and blood money in his pocket! There the man stood, bold as brass, waiting for Russ either to enter the gate or move on.

So Russ did neither. He reversed his direction and walked past to meet Idaho head-on.

The man wasn't expecting it. He backed a few steps, then turned and moved south along the Hill Street walk. He looked over his shoulder, saw Russ gaining and quickened his pace. He crossed Eighteenth with Russ half a block behind.

At the Opera House corner the gap was barely thirty yards. To widen it Idaho broke into a dog trot. A smile straightened Hyatt's lips and he felt better now. The chaser was being chased. He kept on after his man and halfway to Sixteenth saw him dart into the alley back of the Inter-Ocean Hotel.

Crossing that alley Russ looked down it but Idaho wasn't in sight. A dozen steps further on was the hotel's Hill Street door. Russ turned in there, feeling dizzy and faint. He'd walked too fast but he wasn't sorry. Hunting the hunter had released a pressure inside of him.

"I want a room," he said to the desk man. "One with a bolt on the door."

When the bolt was bolted he went to bed and slept eight hours.

The window was dark when he wakened and night sounds came from the streets. The sounds of carriage wheels and gay talk meant that the upperworld of Cheyenne was already theater-bound. Russ lost no time getting downstairs. The lobby clock said eight and the dining room was almost full. John Chase didn't allow guns in the dining room and Russ couldn't risk unstrapping his own. Not with Idaho around.

So he took supper at Ramsey's, a door or two west. Idaho didn't look in on him. Nor was he in sight when Russ left the restaurant and looked both ways along Sixteenth. Common sense told Russ he'd better stay out of dark corners, at least until he heard from Skeets Carson. The smart thing would be to stay behind a bolted door till morning.

But a force stronger than discretion pulled Russ the other way. Pride wouldn't let him skulk or hide.

Instead he walked up Hill to the Opera House corner to mingle in a crowd there. Carriages were still pulling up, bringing late arrivals. There were men in full dress, the club crowd, each with an expanse of hard white shirtfront. "Herefords" was Colonel Murrin's jocular name for them. There were ladies in low-necked gowns, ivory shoulders gleaming under the sidewalk lamps.

The Warrens drove up, dismissed their carriage and went in. Francis Warren, merchant, banker, sheepman, was already rivaling Joe Carey as the top political power in Wyoming. "The greatest shepherd since Abraham," a Chicago daily had called him. After the Warrens came the genial giant Hi Kelly, his hooded Indian wife shy under the gaze of the crowd, Kelly himself as homespun as on the day he'd first cracked a whip over an overland stage. Rumor had it that he'd soon sell out his Chugwater ranch holdings to one of the Swan companies, then move to Cheyenne to run for sheriff and build for his wife the finest mansion west of Omaha.

Russ watched restlessly for Gail Garrison. She was almost the last to come and her gloved hand was on the arm of Gerald Lorton. They'd walked the three blocks from her house, the sidewalk crowd parting to let them through. Russ could have touched her—she passed so close. She didn't see Russ but Lorton did. Lorton was bare-headed, a knee-length opera cape over his shoulders. His steel-green eyes blinked with an odd look of surprise as they met Hyatt's.

Why, Russ wondered, would he be surprised? *He knows I'm riding herd on him.*

When the Opera House filled up the sidewalk crowd drifted away to the hotels and bars. There was a gas lamp on this corner and Russ moved down Seventeenth to be out of its glow. Street lamps were a block apart, the mid-block walks dark except where saloon fronts threw out light. A man in mid-block would make a poor target.

So for a while Russ kept to the gloom of this saloonless block, his back to a blank wall, his eyes alert both ways for Idaho. He had a feeling the man was watching him, waiting for Russ to frame himself against light. If Idaho could kill with one shot, he could dart off down some dark alley and be safe.

Again a swell of anger swept through Russ as he thought of Gerald Lorton, right now snug in a box with Gail Garrison. Snug and smug as he waited there for a hireling to kill Russ Hyatt. Why had he been surprised to see Russ? Was it because he'd thought Russ already dead? After today's encounter on the club porch he knew Russ knew he was Lou. It would make the killing doubly urgent. It would put spurs on murder. More than likely Lorton had sent word to Idaho, through Grimes, demanding quick action and offering a bonus for it.

And what about Grimes? Was he too at the Opera House?

Looking half a block west Russ could see the Carey Block. Its bank floor was dark; so was its upper floor except for one yellow window. Was it the window of Grimes' office?

It overlooked Ferguson and was the third window from Seventeenth. The street lamp was on the opposite corner, in front of the post office. Russ moved that way, trying to remember the exact position of Grimes' office. Maybe Grimes was up there now.

The windowpane showed the silhouette of a man at a desk. The figure's short bulk suggested Wally Grimes, and Russ moved still nearer to be sure.

The shot came just as he reached the corner. A bullet whistled by and Russ feigned a hit, dropping prone on the board walk as he whipped out his gun. The shot came from the north, about thirty steps up the Ferguson Street walk. Lumber was piled there ready for the building of a house. A second shot boomed from the lumber pile and Russ fired at the flash.

He himself was exactly between the gunman and a street lamp back of him, across at the post office. Had it been planned that way? Russ heard shouts and a police whistle as people rushed out of the Delta Club, in the next block south. A third shot came from the lumber pile and again Russ fired at the flash. He couldn't see Idaho, only the flames of his gun.

The police whistle was Constable Nolan's and on his heels came Sheriff Seth Sharpless. In their wake rushed a stampede of the curious who'd burst forth from saloons and gambling clubs at the sound of gunfire.

Russ was getting to his feet as Nolan laid a hand on his arm. "What's going on?" the constable demanded. "Who you cuttin' loose at?" echoed Sheriff Sharpless.

Russ glanced across the street and saw that Grimes' office window was now dark. Had it been lighted as a decoy, to lure him here and set him up for the kill?

"His name's Idaho," Russ told the officers. "He opened up on me from behind that lumber."

With a county officer on one side of him and a city officer on the other, Russ walked to the lumber pile for a look. Nolan struck a match and its flicker showed them a man. He lay face up and didn't move. The face was Idaho's.

Sharpless stooped to feel for a heartbeat. There wasn't any. "You beaned him, mister, and he's dead."

Delving into the dead man's pocket for an identification the sheriff found an envelope with money in it. "Three hundred dollars," he announced after a count.

"Guess I'll have to lock you up," the sheriff said. His grip tightened on Russ Hyatt's arm.

10

As they walked him two blocks up Ferguson to the courthouse, Russ did some fast thinking. If he told about Grimes and a padded cattle tally, they'd let him off. For it would outrage the WSGA, whose political power here was all but dictatorial, and their quick investigation would be sure to uncover the fraud of Wally Grimes. To promote his deal Grimes had referred Miles Cortney to the banks and to leading stockmen. To these Cortney had shown his sale memo mainly to ask if prices per head were fair. Yes, they'd told him, after noting the prices per head were exactly the same as those in other deals.

And while the total number of cattle listed might have seemed high, a reference glancing at the tally list wouldn't question it after noting the initials of two roundup foremen, both trustworthy. Also, herds had been changing hands so fast this past boom year that no banker, or even the WSGA secretary himself, could keep track of just how big each brand was at a given time.

Just the same someone was sure to remember his impression of a high tally if Russ accused Grimes. Cortney would be searched for and the WSGA itself would make a tight check on the Boxed M herd.

If I talk they jug Grimes instead of me. That certainty, churning in Hyatt's brain, was echoed by another. *If I talk it means a coffin for Cortney.*

So with the chips down he couldn't talk. Not yet. All he could claim was self-defense. He'd been opened up on from the dark and had fired back. The name of Grimes couldn't even be mentioned.

At Nineteenth the two officers took him into the courthouse. "City jail's full," the sheriff said, "so we'll have to book you here."

"Which is the best?" Russ asked, forcing a grin.

Sharpless chuckled. "County jail's the best, according to that New York gal who's been writing us up."

At this, City Constable Nolan took quick exception. "No such thing. She gave yours a worse black eye than she did mine."

A deputy took charge of Russ to book him and to list the articles found in his pockets. While the listing was being made the argument went on between Nolan and the sheriff.

"Here's word-for-word what she said about *your* jail," Sharpless cited. " 'The Cheyenne city jail is a horrible, dark, dirty, noisy kennel, unfit for dogs.' "

"Oh yeh?" Nolan jibed back. "But from there she went on to say the county jail's even worse. Listen!" He fished from his pocket a clipped paragraph first printed in the New York *Globe-*

Sun, under the by-line of Jean Markle, and reprinted in a Cheyenne daily. To the confusion of the sheriff, Nolan read bits of it aloud while they were booking Hyatt.

> The county jail, in the courthouse, is an iron cage twenty feet wide, thirty feet long, eight feet high, set in the middle of a room thirty-five feet square. Within this cage is an iron box divided into ten cells, each five by seven feet. Often these ten kennels contain as many as thirty prisoners, with their slop buckets. After a month's confinement, a prisoner is pale, weak and diseased. Some die in the filth there.

Nolan looked up from his reading. "There's a lot more of it. It gets worse as it goes on. I'll leave it to anyone if she didn't give your tramp-trap a worse send-off than she did mine."

The prospect sickened Russ and almost made him change his mind. By sending for Mayor Carey, who also happened to be top man in the WSGA as well as president of a bank, he could blow the lid off and maybe avoid spending even one night in jail.

But again a thought of Cortney muzzled Russ. "You want a lawyer?" a deputy asked him.

"Send for Clem Harwood, the freighter," Russ

decided. "I'll get Clem's advice about a lawyer."

"We'll get word to him," the deputy promised as he led Russ down a corridor to the cage room.

Russ looked at it and his lips drooped. It was exactly as described by Jean Markle. Every box but one had at least two prisoners, and a few had three. One box, near the center, was empty.

The deputy said something but Russ couldn't hear him. There was too much noise. The place rang with moans and sobs and profane songs. Flesh smells nauseated Russ as the deputy put him in the one empty box. A half-crazy Negro in the next one chanted at the top of his voice: "Lawd save us! What I seen once I don' wanna see no mo'! You-all better stay out of that'n, mistah."

"Are you talkin' to me?" Russ asked through the bars.

"It's de wickedest place since Sodom and Gomorrah!" the Negro wailed. "It ain't Hell-on-Wheels no mo'; it's Hell-on-Hossback, jest lak de lady say!"

"Don't pay any attention to him," the deputy advised before leaving. "That sob-sister from New York's got him talkin' to himself."

"Talking about what?"

"About Cheyenne."

His five-by-seven cell had no cot, only a pallet of dirty blankets on its floor. He sat on a stool, his cowboy pride stinging, his will putting a clamp on it for the sake of Cortney. Where was Skeets Carson all this time? In case something happened to Skeets, maybe he'd better confide in Clem Harwood. "It's Hell-on-Hossback!" the Negro kept chanting.

From which Russ gathered that Jean Markle had rechristened this town, changing one word only. "Hell-on-Wheels" was the name it had answered to, these last fourteen years, ever since the U.P. had laid rails through here.

"He's nuts!" a white prisoner jeered from another box. "You are too, brother, fer lettin' 'em stick you in that one."

"That's why it's empty," another man wheezed. "We'd ruther double up, than to be put where *you* are!"

"It's baid luck, mistah!" mourned the Negro. He rolled his eyeballs toward Hyatt's box. "It's baid luck and de debbil hisself!"

"Why?" Russ asked them.

The wheezing man explained. "That one you're in, brother, is the one Mosier had. They snatched him out of it, just a week ago tonight, and drug him off kickin' and screamin'."

"Drug him off an' hung him!" cried the Negro. "Lawd save us! I wish I was in Sodom an' Gomorrah, 'stead of heah in Cheyenne!"

Shortly before midnight the performance of *La Belle Coquette* ended and the audience poured out of the Opera House, some to waiting carriages, others strolling toward nearby homes and hotels. Gerald Lorton came out with Gail Garrison and they turned north up the Hill Street walk. "Wasn't Fay Templeton wonderful!" Gail exclaimed.

Lorton didn't hear her. Her hand resting on his arm felt a sudden tension. Lorton was staring at someone in the street, a thickset man with a broad, fleshy face. He was a ranch owner Gail knew slightly, and rather disliked although she couldn't explain why. She'd met him once or twice at the club and there was something about him she couldn't quite trust. Wallace Grimes was his name.

She saw Grimes take off his hat and fan himself, which seemed a silly thing to do in the cool of midnight. The man was looking right at them. He seemed flushed and excited, yet sober enough. Then he turned and disappeared into the dark.

Lorton continued to be preoccupied all the way to Gail's house. It annoyed her a little. Usually, after a theater date, she asked Gerry in for a cup of coffee. This time she didn't. At the door she turned to him and said: "It was a dandy show, Gerry. Goodnight."

Lorton turned east on Twentieth and stopped at a cottage just across from the public school. The place had a picket fence and geraniums in the front yard. It belonged to a Goshen Hole ranch couple who used it only in the winter, renting it during summer and fall to Gerry Lorton. Lorton kept bachelor quarters here, taking most of his meals at the club.

The porch was dark except for a glowing cigar. Lorton didn't need to be told who was waiting there. He'd caught Grimes' signal. Something big was afoot, to make Grimes waylay him as he left the Opera House.

"Well? What happened?"

"Sudden death," Grimes said huskily.

"Hyatt's?"

"No. Idaho Brown's."

Lorton swore under his breath. "You mean Idaho missed him?"

"Three times. And then took a slug in the head."

Lorton made himself a cigaret, lighting it angrily. "Trust you to mess things up, Wally. Does the law know about it?"

"They were right on top of it, both city and county. They picked Hyatt up and tossed him in the county jail. That's what puts us in a hole, Lou. We're worse off than we were before."

"A lot worse," Gerald Louis Lorton agreed fiercely. He bit on his cigaret, thinking hard. Down at Tucson, Arizona, Grimes had known him as G. Louis Lorton; here in Wyoming he signed checks as Gerald L. Lorton.

"Hasn't opened his trap yet," Grimes said.

"But he will," Lorton predicted, "if he stays in that pesthole very long. I don't care how much he wants to protect Cortney. No man alive can stand that cage even a week, waiting for trial, if he can get out just by opening his mouth."

"But what can we do?" Grimes fretted. "We can't get at him while he's in jail."

"So we've got to get him out!" Lorton snapped, his steel-green eyes bright in the dark. "Fast! Before he gets a bellyful of that stink-hole and starts talking."

"How?"

Lorton shook off his opera cape and sat on the porch rail. "First, tell me just what happened. And where."

Grimes gave a sketchy account of tonight's gunfight. "It looked like a cinch, Lou. Idaho in the dark, back of a lumber pile; Hyatt framed against the corner street lamp."

"Here's what you do," Lorton decided. "Go to the sheriff right now. Rout him out of bed. Say you were in your Carey Block office when it happened. Which is true. You looked out the window and saw the whole thing, which is also true. The first thing you saw was a flash from the lumber pile. A man south along the walk was being shot at. He didn't even have his gun out. In the dark you couldn't make out who he was. A second flash came from the lumber pile and then the other man began shooting back. You swear you saw it just that way."

Grimes mopped beads from his face and squirmed. "I *did* see it just that way, Lou. But I don't like it. I don't want to get mixed up in it."

"You'll be mixed up in it a lot worse—if he tells the court about Cortney."

"But I don't like to . . ."

"Stop stalling, Wally. Do as I say. You cross me and I'll do a little telling myself. To Manuel and Ernesto."

The names had a quick effect on Grimes. "All right," he promised shakily. "I'll go to the sheriff and tell him I saw the flashes just like you say. But after they turn Hyatt loose, what then?"

"You know where Morton's Pass is?"

Grimes nodded. "It's at the head of Sybille Creek, about thirty miles north of the Boxed M."

"How many men could you get there in, say, fifteen hours?"

"Spoffard and Gebbs are at the ranch. Sid and Jonas are helping Jud and Alf. Shorty Goss is tallyin' at the roundup."

"Three or four ought to be enough. Now listen. And this time don't mess it up." Lorton lowered his voice to give terse, precise instructions.

Grimes gaped his approval. "I should've thought of it myself, Lou."

"You should have. But you didn't. How's the deal with the Apperson brothers coming along?"

At this Grimes brightened a little. "They're ripe," he reported. "Been working on them ever since we lost Cortney. Had 'em out to the ranch and it looks good to 'em. I've shown 'em the tally book and they've swallowed it hook and sinker. Money to burn, those boys, and they can hardly wait to spend it on steers."

"Where's Judnick?"

The small eyes of Wally Grimes narrowed slyly. "He's on his way here with a newspaper dated yesterday and signed by both Cortney and Skeets. I'll show it to Hyatt soon as we get him out of jail. He'll sure look sick when he finds out we picked up Skeets!"

"You'll show him nothing," Lorton corrected sharply. "Let him think Skeets is still tracking the buckboard."

Grimes stared, his loose mouth hanging open. Always his slower wits had been a turn behind Lorton's. "Why can't I show it to him? Two hostages are better than one. Skeets is his buddy. He'll keep his mouth shut as long as he thinks . . ."

"Wait till you hear the rest of it," Lorton cut in, and for the first time tonight he smiled. Again he lowered his voice, speaking in brittle whispers, adding final details to his instructions. "Now get going," he finished, "and rout the sheriff out of bed. I want Hyatt freed from jail before noon tomorrow."

When Grimes was gone Lorton went inside, lighted a lamp and poured himself brandy. Sipping it made him remember a julep he'd dropped, about twelve hours ago, on the club porch. Dumb of him to do that! But actually it proved nothing. At best it only bolstered a guess Hyatt had already made.

Guessing isn't proving. And even proof would have no teeth in it. For although G. Louis Lorton had left Tucson under a cloud, he wasn't wanted for any crime there. Or anywhere else. For that matter, neither was Wally Grimes.

It wasn't the law Grimes was afraid of, but two brothers-in-law named Manuel and Ernesto Gonzales. For Grimes, during his Tucson residency, had married a rich *hacendada* in Chihuahua. Tiring of her, he'd deserted her after arranging to have her cattle driven north across the border. With the money the cattle brought, Grimes had continued on north to Cheyenne, there running into an old Arizona neighbor Lou Lorton. He'd asked Lorton's advice about investing the money—and Lorton had sold him the Boxed M brand by padded book tally.

Gerald Lorton sipped his brandy, smiling as he remembered Wally's bleats when the next roundup had exposed the padding. Yet he hadn't dared set the law on Lorton. For Lorton could send word to the deserted Mexicana. She wouldn't be able to extradite Grimes; she couldn't even prove in court that he'd stolen her cattle. All she could prove was desertion. But she had two brothers. The brothers had long memories, pepper-hot resentments and sharp knives. For two years they'd been looking for Wallace Grimes.

It gave Lorton a whip hand over Grimes. And lately he'd used it. Lay off the Boxed M crew, he'd told Grimes in July, and take on a new one, adding to it the half-dozen men who'd helped drive the Mexico herd north across the border. Then pad the tally book and sell out to some ranch-hungry investor from the east. Whatever you clean up, split with me.

It made an out for Grimes. It made a chance to get his money back and slip away well-heeled to a spot where he need no longer fear either Lou Lorton or the brothers Gonzales.

All had gone well until the prospective investor, Miles Cortney, sent for a cowboy who'd once guided him on a hunt. Russ Hyatt. Hyatt who'd know at a glance that the tally was padded.

All would still go well with Hyatt dead.

Gerald Lorton set the teeth of his wits hard on that fact. He finished his drink. Then he looked at a Union Pacific timetable to see when the next train left for Laramie.

11

When Gail Garrison came down to breakfast only her Aunt Matilda was there. Her father was at the Cross D, nearly two hundred miles west, busy with the fall gather in roundup District Number Eight. Only Gail and her aunt and a cook were at the Cheyenne house. And this morning the cook had already relayed Cheyenne's latest sensation to the aunt.

"Another shooting, Gail," the aunt sighed, "and barely three blocks from here. It happened while you were at the theater last night."

"Anyone we know, Aunt Matilda?"

"I don't think so, dear. Just two cowboy gunmen. One killed and the other in jail. Cook says he used to ride for the Boxed M. A man named Hyatt."

Gail looked up, startled. "Hyatt? Which one was . . . ?" The word "killed" stuck in her throat. But it was sure to be Russ Hyatt. Twice lately he'd been shot at, once from ambush on the range and once at a hotel.

"It's Hyatt who's in jail," the aunt told her calmly. "As well he should be! Shooting a man dead right across from Joe Carey's bank! When will our streets be safe?"

Gail's appetite deserted her. In a few minutes

she went out to the stable. "Saddle Brownie for me, please." She hurried back to the house and put on a riding skirt.

After the stableman had helped her to a perch on Brownie's sidesaddle, Gail rode not toward the courthouse but northeast toward the fairgrounds. For days she'd felt an urge to see Clem Harwood. Before going into the freighting business Clem had been wagon boss at the Garrison ranch and as a growing girl Gail had been on a chummy basis with him. Often she'd slipped down to the wagon sheds to hear Clem tell salty tales of his Indian-fighting days.

Just a week ago this morning she'd heard a cry from his cabin near the fairgrounds. She'd failed to investigate and had been sorry for it ever since. Certain things needed explaining and she wanted to talk them over with Clem Harwood. Odd things like moosehide laces from Harwood's boots found tied in hard knots around Russ Hyatt's wrists and ankles. Little things like yesterday morning when from her window she'd seen Hyatt stop at her gate, hand on latch as though coming in, then change his mind and walk away. Why?

Clem Harwood's saddled pony, the one he used to ride back and forth to his freighting corrals, was tied by the cabin. Gail left her mare at the same hitchpost and knocked on the door.

"Bless my life if it ain't Sweetness from

Sweetwater!" Delighted, Clem Harwood took her hand and led her inside, Gail lifting her long riding skirt to step over the sill. Harwood, a small man whose long white hair made him look older than his sixty years, made her comfortable in his one rocker. "Had breakfast yet, young lady? I was jest fixin' to . . ."

"Uncle Clem," she broke in, "do you know Russ Hyatt's in jail? He drove for you one winter, didn't he? Last night he killed a man in a gunfight."

"You don't say!" Clem puckered his mouth judicially. "I'll 'low the other fella had it comin'. Russ is a good boy and he don't shoot 'less'n he's shot at."

Gail told him about her ride around the fairgrounds track a week ago, with Glen Van Tassen, when they'd heard a cry from this cabin. "Van didn't think it was any of our business, so we didn't come over here. But after what happened I feel sure it was Russ Hyatt. Tho' he won't admit it."

"If he says he wasn't here, he wasn't," Harwood argued.

"But *someone* was here! And Russ was found tied with laces probably stolen from your boots. Don't you have any ideas at all?"

"Sure I have. Plenty. They didn't take anything 'cept the boot laces, but they left plenty of sign. Four or five men was here, I figger. One come durin' the night and slept in a bunk. Next mornin' he had callers and they was here nigh all day, judgin' by the mess they left. Two fellas who smoked cigarets and one who smoked cigars and one who dropped pipe ashes all around. They left in a narrow-tired wagon. A ranch buckboard, I figger. Tire prints I found outside measure two inches fer the hind wheels and one and a half fer the front." Reading sign was like reading a book for Harwood.

"If we only knew whose buckboard it was!" Gail murmured.

The freighter grinned. "Who says we don't? They's only four livery stables in town and I checked at all of 'em. Asked 'em who tuk out a two-hoss rig with that size tires about sundown the day them fellas was here. Only one such rig was tuk out that particular evenin'. Charley Chareton of the Bon Ton remembers it. A Boxed M buckboard belongin' to Wally Grimes."

Grimes! The name stirred an uneasy memory in Gail. Last night as they'd left the Opera House! Grimes in the street fanning himself with his hat in the cool of midnight! When she mentioned it, Clem rounded his lips again. "Sounds like he was signallin' somebody."

An answer poised on Gail's lips but she bit it back. The man had been looking straight at them. And Gerry Lorton, on the walk home, was preoccupied and unresponsive. With a start Gail remembered something else. Gerry Lorton had once owned the Boxed M himself.

"The place where Russ got run over by a stampede," Harwood put in, "is on the way to the Boxed M. It ain't the shortest way, but you could get there by drivin' up Pole Crik. Wally Grimes smokes cigars. Humph! So he was giving the high sign to somebody right after the gunfight last night!"

A horseman galloped up Dodge Street and dismounted in front. They heard him knock at the cabin door.

When Harwood opened it a deputy sheriff was standing there. "Hi, Clem. Guy in the hoosegow wants to see yuh. Name of Hyatt. He got too handy with a gun last night and killed a man."

"Tell him I'll be right there," Harwood promised. As the deputy rode away he turned back to Gail with a puzzled look. "What d'yuh reckon Russ wants?"

Her eyes sparked with a thought. "He worked for Wallace Grimes till after the spring roundup. Then Grimes laid off his crew and got another one. It was Grimes' buckboard, you say! There *must* be a connection, Uncle Clem."

"And maybe he wants to let me in on it." Clem Harwood slapped on a hat. "So I better hit fer the jail."

"I'll go with you," the girl insisted.

Harwood eyed her curiously. "He a perticular friend of yourn?"

"I hardly know him," Gail said as they went out to the horses. "But somehow I feel involved. I heard his cry for help and didn't do anything about it. Yesterday he came to my house and changed his mind at the gate. And I want to know why Grimes . . ." Again Gail checked the words. What she really wanted to know was why Grimes had looked straight at Gerry Lorton last night, fanning himself with a hat.

She put her foot in Clem's hand and he lifted her to the sidesaddle. They made an odd pair riding down Dodge Street—the blond girl in her trailing skirt and the wagon boss with his shaggy white hair.

At Nineteenth they turned west and rode to the courthouse corner. Harwood helped Gail down and they went up the steps together. "You better wait here," Harwood said in the hallway. "It's a dirty hole, that cage back there. One whiff and you'd have nightmares for a week. You jest wait here while I . . ."

"No, by all means let her see it!" The cool, accusing voice of Jean Markle broke in and they turned to face her. "It *is* a dirty hole, Miss Garrison, a disgrace to civilization. Go take a look at it, and see what goes on while you dance at the Cheyenne Club and attend operas."

For only a moment Gail took offense. Then

something fine and sincere in the other girl won her over. Impulsively she held out her hand. "You're Jean Markle, aren't you? I've read every one of your articles—about our wealth and wickedness. At first they made me mad. Then they made me ashamed. Some of us really *have* a social conscience. Only it's been asleep. I hope you can wake it up."

The severity faded from Jean Markle's dark, vivid face as she took Gail's hand. "You make *me* feel ashamed. I had no idea you were like this. Won't you forgive me, Miss Garrison?"

Gail smiled. "How did you know my name?"

"I was at the show myself last night," Jean confessed, "and I asked who was that beautiful golden blonde, in the box with the handsome man? You'll forgive me for preaching?"

The Wyoming girl laughed. "I needed it. And please call me Gail." Harwood had left them to go back to the cage. "You're here to do another piece about our jails? Your last one gave me the shivers."

"Not exactly," Jean said. "I came to interview a cowboy who was arrested last night."

Gail's face clouded again. "Russ Hyatt? Do you know him?"

"Not really. But I met him at the hotel just after he'd witnessed the Mosier lynching. Not as a participant but only as a passer-by. Since then

Mosier's cell has been empty—until last night when they put Hyatt into it."

At Gail's confused glance Jean explained: "It gives me an angle of emphasis for a follow-up on the lynching. Don't you see? Man dragged from cell and lynched. Passer-by witnesses lynching. Week later same passer-by put in same cell. How does it feel, Mr. Passer-by?"

"You mean you asked Russ Hyatt that?" Gail gasped.

"I came here to ask him that. But while I was doing it they took him out of the cage and upstairs."

"To the courtroom?"

"No. I went up there supposing it was the usual preliminary hearing. It's not. Something's up. They're in chambers behind a locked door."

"That's right, Gail." It was Clem Harwood rejoining them. "Seems an eyewitness showed up. Him and the J.P. and the D.A. and the sheriff and Russ are in a huddle about it. Looks like a break for Russ."

"Here he comes now," Jean announced, facing the stairs.

They saw Russ Hyatt coming down them, tousled after his night in the cage but grinning cheerfully. "Mornin', folks. Where'd you pick up these good-lookin' gals, Clem?"

"You're free?" the two girls asked in a breath.

"Free as a bird. And hungry as a coyote. They

brought me breakfast but I couldn't whip up an appetite for it in that county kennel. Soon as I wash up, what do you say we all go someplace and eat?"

"We accept," Jean Markle said promptly, scenting good copy for her next in a series called "The Shame of Cheyenne." "Don't we, Gail?"

Gail nodded, smiling. Russ Hyatt would tell Harwood everything, she hoped, and she'd be right there to hear it. A deputy came up to them with a bulky bundle. "Here you are, cowboy. It's the stuff we took off you last night."

Russ reclaimed his gun, cartridge belt, wallet, keys—and a folded bit of dainty silk. With a half-embarrassed grin he handed the little handkerchief to Gail. "You dropped it at the TOT gate. Been waitin' for a chance to give it to you."

Gail's blue eyes gazed up at his quizzically. "Why didn't you, then, when you came to my house yesterday? You got as far as the gate and turned back."

"Lost my nerve, I guess," Russ evaded. But he wasn't a man to lose his nerve and Gail knew it. What was he hiding?

Harwood asked, "Howcome they turned you loose, boy?"

Russ shrugged. "Eyewitness turned up. He saw the other fella shoot first. Saw him shoot twice before I cut loose myself."

"Who is this eyewitness?" Clem prodded.

"What difference does it make?" Again Russ was evasive but this time the answer came from another source. The deputy who'd delivered the pocket articles was still standing by. "Man named Grimes," the deputy said.

Grimes again! More and more Gail was determined to know the truth. She sensed an uneasiness in Russ Hyatt, as though he hadn't wanted the name Grimes to come up. He said nothing as they went out to the sidewalk. And yet Gail's first guess—that Grimes was hostile to Hyatt—seemed to be all wrong. For a volunteered testimony from Grimes had freed Russ from jail.

"You invited us to eat with you," Gail reminded him, "and we're not going to let you wiggle out of it. Where shall we meet you?"

"Inter-Ocean dining room," Russ said, "soon as I've cleaned up."

"Jean, my house is only a block from here. Come along with me while I change." To the men Gail added, "We'll be there in half an hour."

The portly John Chase himself ushered them to a table. Gail had changed to a street dress and Russ had been to his room for a bath and a shave. Clem Harwood wore a puzzled look, as though Russ in their half hour alone together had told him a little, but not all. It wasn't quite noon and only Russ Hyatt was hungry.

Gail, who'd come to listen and not to eat, was

quickly baffled and disappointed. Russ sidestepped every trap she laid for information.

She gave a helpless gesture. "Isn't he maddening, Jean? He shouted for help and I heard him. Now he denies being there at all."

"I didn't deny being anywhere," Russ hedged. "I just said I didn't yell for help. Let's talk about last night's show. Was it pretty good?"

"Let's talk about Grimes," Gail said stubbornly. "And his narrow-tired buckboard; and moosehide laces."

Clem Harwood, thoughtfully cooling his coffee in a saucer, followed up with: "How did you get out of that buckboard, boy, all tied up with my boot laces?"

Watching Russ, Gail decided he was torn between two impulses. An impulse to confide in them and some compelling restraint. His eyes were on constant alert. Several times he started to say something and didn't. More than once he glanced through a window at people on the walk, as though fearful of being watched. His light talk, Gail sensed, was only a cover-up for some life-or-death tension.

"One of us is getting a telegram," Jean Markle said.

A boy from the depot spoke to a waiter who pointed toward Russ Hyatt. "Message for you, mister." The boy handed a yellow envelope to Russ, took his tip and went his way whistling.

" 'Scuse me," Russ said as he took out the message.

Reading it, an iron-red excitement overspread his face. His eyes sparked as he stood up. "This is kinda what I've been waitin' for, folks. Got to get my bronc and ride. I'll pay the tab as I go out. Clem, you take care of these ladies and see they get home all right."

"No bad news, I hope?" Jean murmured.

"No ma'am. It's more like good news." Russ looked at Gail. "Sorry to romp off like this. But I can't fool around any. Got to do sixty miles by noon tomorrow."

As he left the table Harwood called after him, "If you need an outfit, stop by my cabin and help yourself."

"Thanks," Russ called over his shoulder. Gail saw him stop at the lobby desk, lay money on it and speak to the clerk. He took his gunbelt from a rack and went out by the Hill Street door.

"How do you like *that?*" Gail exclaimed to Jean. "We've been walked out on. First date he ever had with us, too." She turned seriously to Harwood. "He *must* have told you *something,* Uncle Clem. You were alone with him half an hour."

"All I could get out of him," Harwood confided, "is that a pard of his is in a fix. A danged tight fix. If it leaks out, this pard of his'll be a dead pigeon. Just one whisper to a sheriff, or anyone else, and his pard stops breathin'."

The girls stared. "Did he say anything else?" Gail asked.

"Not a word, Gail. And you'd better not either. We better sit tight on this till we hear from Russ. He's been shot at enough already. Wonder who that pard of his is!"

"Maybe he's the one who sent the telegram," Jean suggested.

"Like as not," Clem brooded. "Wonder what it said!"

An idea brought Jean to her feet. "Come, Gail. Let's go find out."

"Ain't no way you can find out," Harwood argued. "Them telegrams are confidential. You go over to the depot, they won't tell you a thing."

"Anyway thanks for everything, Uncle Clem," Gail said. The girls went out to the street where Gail's buggy was tied. They'd driven to the hotel in it after leaving Gail's saddle mare at the Garrison stable.

"What Uncle Clem doesn't know," Jean said as they got into the buggy, "is that I'm the day operator's best customer. I've been filing copy with him nearly every day, to the *Globe-Sun* in New York."

Gail clucked her horse toward the depot. "You think we can corrupt him?" she asked hopefully.

"We can try. It was he," Jean added with a smile, "who took me to *La Belle Coquette*."

"That should make it simple." Gail touched her horse with a whip and they turned west on Fifteenth.

"I filed another long dispatch early this morning," Jean said. "And by the way, as I was filing it I saw your handsome, fair-haired escort of last night. He was getting on a westbound train."

"That would be Number 3 due through at seven o'clock. So you must be mistaken, Jean. Gerry Lorton never gets up that early."

"This morning be did," Jean insisted. They stopped at the depot and she got out. "You wait here, Gail. I can subdue him better if we're alone."

Jean went in to see her friend the day operator. And Gail, waiting in the buggy, wondered. Why would Gerry leave town on an early train? He hadn't planned a trip. She was certain of that because during the show last night he'd asked her to take a ride with him this morning. A canter out to the fort and back. She couldn't go because her mare Brownie had an eleven o'clock date with Henry Haas to be reshod. But Gerry wouldn't have asked her if he'd planned to catch an early train west.

So he must have planned it *after* they left the show. Could a signal from Grimes have anything to do with it? Grimes who'd freed Russ Hyatt from jail this morning!

Jean's voice brought Gail out of her uneasy thoughts. "It was simple," the New York girl reported gayly. "Nothing secret or sinister about the telegram, he said, so he showed me the file copy and I wrote it down."

She handed Gail a scrap with the words:

> Russ Hyatt
> Inter-Ocean Hotel, Cheyenne,
>   Meet me on Morton's Pass noon tomorrow.
> Skeets.

It had been filed at Laramie, fifty miles west on the railroad.

"Who's Skeets?" Jean asked, "and where's Morton's Pass?"

"Skeets is a friend of his; a TOT rider. Morton's Pass is about sixty miles northwest."

"That fits," Jean remembered. "He mentioned a sixty-mile ride. Let's go tell Uncle Clem."

They drove back to the hotel but Harwood wasn't in the dining room or the lobby. They had him paged in the bar without result. Driving up one street and down another, they wasted an hour looking for the old freighter. Then they tried the corral on O'Neil Street where he kept his teams. "The boss ain't been around," they were told.

"Maybe he went home," Gail said. "Let's go there and see."

Her troubled look made Jean ask: "What's the matter? Have I missed something?"

"I'm thinking of Russ Hyatt. After a night in jail he's in no condition for a ride like that." As a ranch girl Gail knew that sixty miles in a saddle, between two noons over rough country, meant a man-killing, horse-killing pace.

But that was the least of it. Ugly shadows grew in Gail's mind. What if Skeets hadn't sent the telegram! What if a forged message was decoying Russ Hyatt to ambush on a lonely mountain pass!

A telegram from Laramie! Number Three, with Gerald Lorton aboard, had gone to Laramie early this morning. Had Gerry . . . ?

Gail threw off the thought. It was absurd and disloyal. She knew Gerry Lorton. Knew him better than she knew any other man in Cheyenne. Certainly she couldn't take such a wild idea to the sheriff. How could she even mention it to Uncle Clem Harwood? Or to Jean Markle?

12

Russ made the Pole Creek stage station in time for an early supper. Pushing on he left the stage road and bore northwest on a trail leading to upper Horse Creek. He hadn't gone far on it when his mount shied. Dusk was closing in and in the dimness Russ saw an arch of buzzard-picked ribs which had been Tony, his sorrel.

A hard knot of bitterness grew in Russ as he rode on. He had a score to settle with Grimes and Judnick and the rest of them. An especial score to settle with Alford whose sneak bullet had done for Tony. And a still more personal one to settle with Gerald Lorton, smooth, gunless man-about-town, sipping his drinks on the Cheyenne Club veranda while he pulled the strings of murder.

"He's Lou, or I'm a Chinaman!" Russ concluded again.

He rode on with his mind centering on Skeets Carson. Skeets who'd be waiting for him on Morton's Pass, come noon tomorrow. Skeets wouldn't have wired him, Russ thought hopefully, unless he'd located the hideout where they were holding Cortney. Too risky for Skeets to try the rescue alone, so he'd ridden to the nearest rail point, Laramie, to telegraph Russ. "Together we can take 'em," Russ thought. And once Cort was released, they could sick the law on Grimes.

Russ made the Y Bar, on upper Horse Creek, by eleven at night. Only a choreman was there, the others being far to the north on the district roundup. "Hear you been gettin' shot at," the choreman said. "What's the lowdown?"

"Don't know myself," Russ said. "Right now all I need's a four-hour sleep and a fresh horse."

"Help yourself, cowboy."

"Heard from the roundup yet?" Russ asked as he shook off his boots.

"Nope. They'll be gatherin' 'em fer a month yet."

Even then, Russ thought as he lay in the dark waiting for sleep, in many outfits the tallies wouldn't be complete. They'd be complete enough to show up the Boxed M, where the shortage was six-thousand head, but other brands with more normal shortages might not be exposed at all. Some brands made no effort for a complete tally in the fall; all they wanted was to gather a reasonable beef shipment, enough to pay off a bank note or to declare the usual dividend to stockholders. That was why the code of selling by book count could flourish, year after year in Wyoming. As long as regular dividends went out, who cared whether the books were right or wrong?

It couldn't be kept up forever, Russ thought. Someday would come a big freeze, or a deep dive in the livestock market, or both, and the bubble would burst.

He was up and asaddle before daylight. This buckskin the choreman had furnished him with had wind and legs. By daylight Russ had crossed the head of Bear Creek and before the sun was an hour high he made the upper forks of the Chug.

He picked the right-hand fork because it bore toward Morton's Pass. The pass was still eighteen crowflight miles away and getting there by noon would take grim riding. Only because he had a strong fresh horse was there any chance at all. From here on it was up-slope and rough. Rolling prairie was behind and Russ was now in scrub cedar. The Laramie Mountains made a wall in front of him, yellow patches showing there where the cold fall nights had already touched the quakenasp parks.

The carbine on his saddle was the one Skeets had furnished him with, at the TOT. His own had been taken by Judnick and Alford. It made one more reason to hunt them down. He forced the buckskin on. "Step along, Buck. We mustn't keep Skeets waiting."

In mid-morning he left the Chugwater drainage and hit Middle Fork of Sybille. Beyond this the trail twisted upward toward a pass. Russ had gathered Boxed M cattle here. Now he sighted stock of various brands, Boxed M,

LD, Horseshoe, Campstool and Duck Bar. He assumed that the District Number One roundup hadn't yet worked this upper Sybille range.

The cattle petered out as he rode up into pine timber and at the divide there were none at all. He struck the divide in an open glade and from it could see far west across the Laramie Plains. A seldom-used trail from Bosler to Fort Laramie angled northeast along here. Following it a mile or so to the right would put Russ in Morton's Pass. It was a low gap, as mountain passes go, timbered on the north and open on the south.

Russ spurred that way, his ear cocked for a hail from Skeets. As he drew nearer he saw Skeets' horse tied to a sapling in the pass—the white-stockinged black on which Skeets had left the TOT.

The sun was noon high and Russ Hyatt's spirits took a bound. He was here on time. He could hardly wait to ask Skeets where . . .

Russ reined up with a suddenness which pulled the buckskin to its haunches. The noon sun glittered on glass by the trail. The glass was a half-pint bottle with the label side up.

The label said Kentucky Squire whisky!

Alford! Alford who always carried a saddle dram of that brand! Russ stepped to the ground, picked up the bottle and sniffed. The whisky smell was still fresh. So not many hours ago Alford had ridden by here.

There were hoofmarks on the trail. But they proved nothing because occasionally a rider from Bosler to Fort Laramie might pass along here.

And if Skeets was waiting in the pass why didn't he make himself known? Russ, exposed in the open, could easily be seen from the timber there. Yet only silence came from the pass.

Another point hit Russ. He'd warned Grimes that he, Russ Hyatt, had confided in a friend; and that therefore Grimes would gain nothing by setting snipers to kill Hyatt. Yet the warning hadn't stopped Grimes. He'd hired Idaho to kill from the dark. Why had Grimes dared to do that?

Mildly the point had puzzled Russ. Now it puzzled him no longer. Grimes wouldn't worry about Skeets if Skeets was already downed by Judnick and Alford. Skeets, tracking a buckboard, could have followed too close and been gunned. Maybe they'd kill him, or maybe they were holding him alive with Cortney to make two hostages instead of one.

In either case they'd know the friend's name. And could use it in a trick telegram—a lure to bag Russ himself.

It all dovetailed. It explained why Grimes had shown up as an eyewitness at the jail. He wanted Hyatt loose in the woods, not safe behind bars in the courthouse.

Chagrined, Russ stood there in the trail with a half-pint bottle in his hand. He'd be a sitting duck for the Grimes crew if he rode into the brushy pass. It was about two hundred yards to the trees there.

A shot cracked. One instant the bottle was in Hyatt's hand and the next it wasn't. A bullet meant for his heart hit the glass flask, shattered it into chips. In the same breath Russ swung to his saddle. He spurred off to the left, toward a bare, blunt butte about a mile off the trail. A low butte, boulder-strewn on its flat top, with gentle, gravelly slopes on four sides. Russ didn't even reach for his carbine as he rode hard toward it.

Bullets chased him. He lay forward on the buckskin's mane and raced on. Looking back he saw four riders burst from the wooded pass and charge toward him. Their mounts were fresh; his wasn't. In any long race they could run him down. He understood why they hadn't waited for him to ride into the trap. They'd seen him pick up the bottle and knew it gave them away. So one of them had cut loose at two hundred yards, hoping for a one-shot kill.

The butte was low and not steep. Russ pounded up its slope with the buckskin blowing hard. Its flat top had outcroppings, a few of the rocks stirrup-high. Russ hit the ground among them with his carbine out. Then he kneeled back of a rock and triggered lead at four oncoming horsemen.

One of them slumped forward on his pummel.

All of them stopped short, three of them with rifle stocks at cheek, sweeping the hill with bullets. Russ recognized Alford and took aim on the man. Then chips of rock splashed into his eyes, half blinding him; a bullet had caromed from his boulder.

The shock made him miss Alford and he saw three of the riders whirl to move out of range. The fourth horse whinnied, followed with dragging reins with its rider clinging to the saddle.

Well out of range the four went into a huddle, no doubt to plan the safest attack. Russ saw that the fourth man wasn't seriously hurt; when the others helped him to the ground he was able to stand upright. One of them might be the trigger-happy ex-marshal from Kansas, Spot Spoffard.

They'd surround him, Russ reasoned, one man to a side. That way it would be just a question of time. The only water up here was the quart in Russ's canteen. No food, not even fuel for a fire. Otherwise this low, flat-topped hill was a perfect fortress.

While they were deploying, Russ prepared his defense. He unsaddled the buckskin in the center of the summit. The beast's head and ears might be seen by men surrounding the hill, but they weren't likely to shoot at anything except Russ himself.

He spotted a sizable rock near the rim on each of four sides. He'd have to watch from first one, then the other. It seemed hopeless. He took a look and saw that they'd scattered. Trees from the pass came to within three hundred yards of him on the north and in them the slightly wounded man was posted. The others took cover on the west, east and south.

They could wait till dark and then come at him from four directions. Russ's only real hope was to pick them off one by one. He counted his shells. There were thirty-four, giving him none to waste. Given a decent target and time to aim, he could be fairly sure of a hit at two hundred yards; dead sure of it at a hundred.

A chunky man in a gray hat and brown jacket seemed to give the orders. He'd picked cover for the other three. Judnick was posted in a shallow gully to the west and Alford back of a lone, lightning-split snag to the south. The man giving orders was probably the Boxed M foreman, Spoffard. He stationed himself east of the butte in a small island of scrub aspen.

They were deliberate in the deployment, each man taking his post cautiously afoot after leaving his mount beyond his station and out of Hyatt's range. Russ fired twice at Alford and splintered bark from the snag. He shifted for a shot at Judnick and saw the man duck out of sight in his gully. Each of the other two had a brush screen and couldn't be seen.

After a few shots to remind Russ he was

trapped, they did no more shooting. Their least risk would be either to starve Russ out or to attack from four sides during the night. Either way they'd get him. He had a little water for himself but none for his horse. The butte top had no grass to speak of. Unwatered and unfed, the horse would be in no condition for a run if Russ made a break after nightfall.

Again Russ crawled from rock to rock, hoping for targets. Nothing showed except Judnick's face peering out of the gully. As Russ fired the man ducked out of sight. His shot drew no answer.

Slowly the afternoon sun moved across the sky and a hopeless feeling grew on Russ. If he rode or led his horse down a slope, after dark, they'd hear the hoofs crunch gravel and close in on him. His best chance would be to abandon his mount and try to sneak through on foot. If he could get his hands on Judnick's horse, or Alford's, he might outrun them in the dark.

As the sun dipped lower he began planning it that way. He'd free the buckskin, unsaddled, and at once it would start down a slope looking for water. Hoof sounds on gravel might draw all four besiegers that way, while Russ slipped quietly down the opposite slope.

All this while he kept circling his summit hoping for a shot. Not once did Alford show more than an elbow. He caught only brief glimpses of Spoffard. The man in woods to the north fired twice during the late afternoon, proving he was there. The others saved their bullets. The only real chance Russ had for a hit came at sundown, when Judnick raised his head and shoulders above the gully's rim.

Russ let fly at him and again the man dropped out of sight. He didn't yell, so Russ concluded it was a miss.

Through the hour of twilight his thoughts fixed on Miles Cortney. And Skeets. His only chance to keep them alive was to stay on the loose himself. If a bullet found Russ it meant a finish for Cort and Skeets. No one would ever know about Grimes until it was too late. By then Grimes would have found himself another investor, cheating him to the tune of one hundred and eighty thousand dollars.

He himself, Russ admitted with a sick conscience, had also cheated that other investor. Cheated him by silence. If he'd told on Grimes, the fraud would have been nipped in the bud. It would have sacrificed Cortney, but it would have saved Skeets Carson. The thing was even broader than that. Prompt exposure of Grimes would have saved the good name of an industry—the cattle industry of Wyoming. Speculation by book tally would be stopped cold in its tracks—for after the exposure of Grimes every new investor, no matter how eager, would demand a count on the hoof.

It would all come too late if he, Hyatt, met death on this hill.

Unless even after death he could warn them!

Was there a way? Russ took a notebook from his pocket and tore out a blank page. Decision narrowed his eyes. Why not hide a note in the mane of the buckskin horse? He could abandon the horse whose thirst would drive it through the dark to the nearest water. It was a barn-fed horse and a barn horse always goes home. The first Y Bar cowboy who combed the cockleburs from its long tawny mane would find the note. Cort and Skeets and Hyatt might be dead by then, but truth would be out.

He'd address the note to . . . ? That needed thought and Russ, huddling behind a rock as twilight faded, weighed it carefully. The real ruling power in Wyoming was the WSGA. And that giant association of cattlemen had more reason than anyone else to keep the industry clean, and to punish cheaters like Grimes.

Yet Russ knew that the WSGA had two factions. One faction followed the leadership of Alex Swan and did business at the First National Bank. The other took its inspiration from Tom Sturgis and did business at the Stockgrowers' National. The code of trading by book tally had less vogue in the second group than in the first. In fact Tom Sturgis had time and again warned against it. Sturgis was a solid cowman, respected everywhere, and just the man to crack down on Grimes.

Russ wrote on his paper:

To Sheriff Seth Sharpless,
To Tom Sturgis, Sec'y of the WSGA,
To Joe Carey, Pres. Stockgrowers' Nat'l Bank,
    Wally Grimes padded his tally book to show 6000 head too many and got caught at it by me and Miles Cortney. He kidnapped Cortney and Skeets Carson and aims to bury them out of sight soon as he gets me. Right now his gunnies have got me treed on a butte near Morton's Pass.
                        RUSS HYATT.

He wanted to add a line mentioning Lorton. But if he said anything that couldn't be proved, he'd weaken the rest. Nothing could be proved on Lorton. Everything could be proved on Grimes. The fall roundup itself, give it time, would show up Grimes.

The thirsty buckskin stamped restlessly. Russ cut two strands of hair from its long thick mane. These he used to tie the note out of sight under the mane.

The last light faded and gave way to a moonless starlight. Russ didn't dare wait any longer. At the first deep darkness they'd rush him. He made one final round of his battle stations, to listen in case they were creeping up.

All he heard was the champing of his own restless horse.

He'd get in woods quicker if he went to the north and there he'd have only a wounded man to deal with. But he'd need to pick up a mount and one tied in dark woods would be hard to find. Judnick's horse, in the open beyond the gully, would be easier located.

Thought of Judnick sparked another one. Since sundown Russ hadn't seen him at all. Could his sundown shot at Judnick have been a hit? The man's head had dropped out of sight, at the shot, and hadn't reappeared.

He could have been lying dead in the gully for the last two hours. It was a thin chance but Russ took it. He led his horse to the east rim, took off the tie rope and slapped its flank. The buckskin moved off at a running walk downslope, hoofs grinding on gravel.

Right away came a shot from the island of aspens. And Spoffard's voice: "Look out! He's comin'!"

Russ crossed to the opposite rim. He started downslope afoot, rifle at the ready, advancing swiftly through the dark toward Judnick's post on the west.

13

Faintly he heard voices on the other three sides—exchanges between Spoffard and two others. But not a sound from Judnick in the gully.

Then a shout from Spoffard: "It ain't him! It's only his bronc. Get back to your stations and don't let him sneak by."

Russ was now on level ground. He broke into a run and was at the gully before he knew it, almost tumbling in. A dim shape in its bed lay face down. Its arms were outflung and motionless. It could only be Judnick. Judnick dead since sundown!

Alford called shrilly from the south. "Hi there, Jud! He turned his bronc loose. Look out for a trick, Jud."

Judnick's failure to answer might bring them on the run. Russ kneeled by the dead man to take his gunbelt. He picked up a rifle and scrambled out of the gully on its far side. From there he moved fast away from the scene of siege.

"Whatsamatter, Jud?" "He don't answer, Spoff." Voices kept calling from the dark.

The shape of a saddled horse loomed in front of Russ. It was Judnick's horse, tied and ready for pursuit in case Russ tried an escape. He crammed Judnick's carbine in the saddle scabbard and hung Judnick's gunbelt over the horn. Then he mounted and rode off into darkness, doubly armed, dead away from the butte. It was eight hours till daylight and they couldn't follow him in the dark.

Reining left, Russ headed toward Bosler on the U.P. At the first water he stopped to let the horse drink, refilling his canteen. This was a short-coupled brown gelding, young and blockily built. A rolled blanket was tied back of the cantle and maybe Judnick had wrapped a ration or two there. Eighteen hours of steady riding and fighting, since leaving the Y Bar, had famished Russ.

So he opened the blanket roll for a look. Yes, here were bacon and coffee and some hard bread. And a folded newspaper.

Russ remembered a Cheyenne *Leader* Grimes had flashed on him, a dated copy signed by Miles Cortney. A proof that Cort was alive on a certain date. Was this another such proof?

Russ struck a match to see. The paper was two days old. It was the Laramie *Boomerang* published by Bill Nye. Two names were signed across the front page. Miles Cortney. Skeets Carson!

So they had Skeets too! It wasn't a guess any longer but a certain fact. Remorse stung Russ. He himself had sent Skeets into this trap. The only way he could make up for it was to get Skeets, and Cortney, out of it alive.

He should be hot-footing toward Skeets, not away from him. Instead of high-tailing toward town and a snug bed, he ought to push hell-bent into the hills to find Cort and Skeets.

And why should he run away from those gunnies? There were only three of them now at the pass, one of them maybe nicked by a bullet. He, Russ, had plenty of guns and a fresh horse. They wouldn't even look for him in the morning. They'd suppose he'd lit out for some ranch, or for a settlement on the railroad.

So they wouldn't waste time chasing him. Where would they go? Russ chewed on it and decided one of them would ride to Cheyenne, or at least to the Boxed M, and report to Grimes. They'd have to let Grimes know that the ambush had misfired, and that Judnick was dead.

The other two would bury Judnick. Then where? More than likely to the hideout where they held two prisoners. It might be only ten or twenty miles farther into the mountains. If Russ could follow them unseen he'd learn where they were keeping his friends.

But if he rode to town he'd lose them—lose his last and only chance to find Skeets! All thought of retreat left Russ. Instead he followed the water downhill for a mile, then stopped in timber to unsaddle. He tied the horse in bluestem by the creeklet, lighted a fire, made coffee and broiled bacon on a stick.

Then he crawled into a thicket with the blanket. Five hours was all he could allow himself. Long practice had taught him the art of timing his sleep.

It was a sleep of sharp dreams—an iron cage in a jail, gunmen hunting him through the streets of Cheyenne, steers trampling him in the dark—then an alarm clock jangled in his mind and he sat up, pulling on his boots. The angle of a late-rising moon told him the sun would follow in another hour or so.

In a few minutes he was asaddle and heading upcountry. Not toward but away from Cheyenne. One shoulder of Morton's Pass was a wooded peak and Russ knew a game path that would take him there. Once he'd used it as a lookout on roundup, to spot stray bunches of stock. From its top a man could see far in three directions.

Nearing it, steepness made Russ dismount and lead his horse. Light was breaking when he got to the summit. Below him he could see the little flat-topped hill where he'd stood them off yesterday.

Looking east he could see nearly all of the Horse Creek-Chugwater range while to the west the Laramie Plains made a sea of grass to and beyond the Medicine Bow River. Thirty-odd miles to the south he made out a thin column of smoke, perhaps a U.P. engine puffing up Sherman Hill from Laramie. Only to the north and northwest did rugged, timbered mountains wall off distant view.

At sunup Russ saw three mounted men, one of them leading a pack mule. They came out of the trees at Morton's Pass and rode to the little butte just south of it. Russ could see that one of them was riding Skeets' white-stockinged black horse. The rider wasn't Skeets, of course. They'd brought the horse here yesterday merely to make Russ think Skeets was waiting in the pass.

The man on Skeets' horse seemed to have a bandage around his head. He rode off west, leading the mule, dipping into timber which sloped down toward the Laramie Plains.

The other two men rode to the flat top of the butte. Russ saw them pick up his saddle gear. Then they began cleaning up empty cartridges and smoothing out all sign of Hyatt's stand there yesterday. When it was done they headed southeast, toward Cheyenne.

By their hats and mounts Russ knew they were the men he believed to be Spoffard and Alford.

The one man heading west with the pack mule meant more to Russ. The mule could be loaded with supplies for the hideout. The man was out of sight now. But Russ knew his direction of travel. Soon he'd be down to the open prairie. And a mounted man leading a mule can be seen a long way across the Laramie Plains.

Russ led his horse down the game path and

then rode to the butte. Nothing was left there to show there'd been a fight. He rode down to the gully and found it empty. They must have taken Judnick away before daylight and buried him in the woods.

One thing they hadn't taken was the buckskin horse. Right now it ought to be knee-deep in grass on some fork of Sybille. Leisurely it would range homeward toward the Y Bar.

Russ rode the opposite way—toward the spot where a horseman and a led mule had disappeared. It took him into down-sloping timber and in this he made no effort to find hoofprints.

When he came out into the open he was on the edge of the great Laramie Plains which stretched more than a hundred miles west toward the Continental Divide. Two dots far out on it were a horseman and a mule. The man was now angling northwest on a course to strike the Laramie River at Antelope Ford.

Russ rolled a cigaret and slowed his gait. It would spoil everything if the man found out he was being followed.

In mid-morning he crossed the Laramie River. Beyond this the grass stood lush, in spots stirrup-high and waving in the wind. A band of antelope moved through it, far off, like bobbing ducks on a sea. Less than five years ago buffalo had blackened this vast basin of grass; today Russ saw only cattle, range mares and antelope.

He kept an open eye for roundup wagons. The Laramie Plains were roundup District Number Seven with Bob March in charge this year.

Then he reasoned that the man ahead was pretty sure to know where the wagons were just now and would steer clear of them. Russ spotted him about three miles ahead and it looked like he'd hit the Rock River stage road near Badger Flats.

Russ hooked a leg around his saddle horn and thought about two mornings ago, at the jail. And Gail Garrison showing up there! Memory of it brought a half smile to his face. How could she possibly care one way or another? Did she know something? Or suspect something? After all she'd been out with Gerald Lorton the night before. Had something given her a dim hint that Lorton was in it with Grimes?

It was past noon when Russ hit the deep-rutted stage road. He'd seen the man ahead turn north along it. Russ turned that way himself, toward the piney backbone of the Laramie Mountains. He was now about thirty miles north of Rock River on the U.P., and heading toward Mule Creek Pass.

A few miles on he hit the north fork of the Laramie and for a while the trail followed up it. Here scrub timber began and Russ lost sight of the man ahead. Presently he met a freighter with a load of hides for shipment at Rock River. The outfit had stopped to water the six mules of its team. "Hi," Russ said. "I been tryin' to catch up with a guy leadin' a pack mule. Black horse and yellow mule. How far ahead are they?"

"Not fur." The muleteer bit off a chew. "Two-three miles, maybe."

"Thanks." Russ watered his mount and let it rest a few minutes. "Much travel on this trail?"

"Nothin' but the stage and a few freight outfits like mine. There comes one now. Zeke Potter headin' fer Sheridan."

Russ lingered there while Zeke Potter pulled up. He had four horses and a canvas-covered cargo.

"Hi, Ed." The two freighters were old friends.

"Howdy, Zeke. Whatcha haulin' this trip?"

"Twenty barrels of whisky," Zeke said, "and a sack of flour."

"Golly! Whatcha gonna do with all that *flour!*" Ed slapped his knees and bent double, convulsed with his own joke.

Russ grinned and rode on. He increased his pace a little, to close in on the man ahead. The country got brushier with every mile. Unless the hideout was this side of the divide the man would have to make a night camp.

At sundown he was still going. By then the trail was steep, sometimes wooded and sometimes on an open bench or twisting up some dry ravine. Russ closed the gap to less than half a mile.

As the trail got into aspens the ravines began

to show water. The water was still flowing south toward the Laramie Plains. Dusk deepened and the man ahead pushed on. On to Mule Creek Pass and a bit beyond it Russ almost ran into him. He'd stopped to make camp at a seep of water.

Russ drew back half a mile to make one himself.

At daybreak he was fed and ready to go. The other man seemed in no hurry. Russ waited impatiently, spying from the forest. But when the man did start he moved fast, heading down the north side of the range. He crossed the head of La Bonte in a canyon called Old Maid's Draw. A few Duck Bar cows were grazing there.

This was watershed of the North Platte, densely wooded, the trail threading among tiny creeklets each with a succession of beaver dams. When it came out briefly on a bare bench Russ looked below and saw his man and mule. They were pressing steadily on.

Laramie Peak towered at Russ's right and Warbonnet close at his left. A covey of grouse ran across the trail in front of him, scattering in the brush with mellow little whistles. He spurred on down the grade and for the next few miles caught no sight of his man.

In a forest glade called Downey Park the trail leveled for a little way. Russ heard a rattle of trace chains as a Concord stage came swaying toward him across the park. It was a stage line that ran four hundred miles from Custer on the Northern Pacific to Rock River on the U.P.

Russ held up his hand and the driver didn't mind resting his four horses a minute. "How far down did you pass a man leadin' a yellow pack mule?"

"Didn't pass him, neighbor. But I seen him. He was at La Prele fork about twenty minutes ago, turnin' west up La Prele. Giddap." The whip flicked and the stage rolled on.

Russ rode downtrail a few miles to a V fork. There he left the stage road and doubled back southwest, heading toward high country again. From a brow just before he struck La Prele Creek he sighted his man and mule. They were pointing upcreek toward Cold Springs Pass.

So Russ knew they'd turn off short of the pass. There'd be no sense in crossing a divide on one pass only to recross it on another—one which would again lead him down to the Laramie Plains.

Russ kept on and was still within sight when the man ahead turned left off the trail. The one he took was a dim path leading up French Creek. There'd been no general travel on it and Russ easily made out the fresh prints. Dim tire tracks told him that something like a buckboard had passed here. Upcreek the country stood on its head, rising steeply toward Warbonnet.

The creek had willows and a few aspen. Around

two bends of it Russ sighted a cabin. There were sheds and a corral and beyond them a majestic bank of pines slanting upward to the sky. At the main shed a man was loosening the hitch on a pack mule. A man came from the cabin to help him. Something familiar about the second man. Alongside a shed was a buckboard—surely the one which had hauled a prisoner here.

Russ led his mount into brush, crossed the creek just below a beaver dam and made camp in a copse of aspen. He was a good half mile below the cabin. There was no loose stock in sight, or fences, nor any ditch from the creek. It looked like people had started a ranch here and for some reason had deserted it. Indians maybe, or outlaws, or sheer loneliness could have driven them away. And now men in the pay of Wally Grimes had moved in, using the place for a hideout. At the wilderness end of a far, lost trail. They'd be hard to find here.

Russ slipped afoot upcreek through the brush to see what he could see and hear what he could hear. He had a carbine in hand and a holster gun at his thigh.

Two men were hunched on their spurs by a shed. "Yeh, Jonas, we muffed it," one said. "He sneaked through us in the dark and rid back to Cheyenne."

"Wally won't like it, Sid," Jonas predicted, "and neither will Lou." His speech made Russ remember. This was Roy Jonas, wanted in Cheyenne for killing a deputy. A fast man with his guns, they said, and he'd been known to wear two of them. Too fast for a deputy who'd tried to arrest him in an Eddy Street saloon.

Sid twisted a cigaret and hung it from his lip. He'd taken the bandage from his head, so the bullet scratch there couldn't be deep. "How's the boarders?" he asked.

"The dude don't give me no trouble," Jonas said. "But I'd as lief bulldog a steer as handle that other'n. How much longer we gotta keep 'em fer pets?"

"Till we wrap up Hyatt," Sid said. And Russ needed to know nothing more. Skeets and Cort were alive and close by.

He raised his carbine and drew a bead on Jonas. Then a whisper of caution stirred in his mind. He'd better count saddles. Five of them were draped on the corral fence. One was a saddle Sid had just taken from a white-stockinged black horse. Another Russ recognized as his own— one he'd checked at the IXL barn in Cheyenne. Alford had called there for Hyatt's outfit to make people think he'd left town to guide Cortney on a hunt.

Three other saddles on the corral fence meant that three outlaws were here. Jonas and Sid and one other. The third man must be close by, maybe in the cabin. He'd better not start shooting,

Russ decided, until he had them all bunched.

Night would be the time. Or mealtime when they were all three in line at a table. Russ withdrew quietly into the creek brush, to watch and wait. He couldn't risk a slip. Nothing less than a clean sweep would save his friends.

14

One hundred and thirty crowflight miles southeast of French Creek, the richest and wickedest city on earth (according to Jean Markle of the New York *Globe-Sun*) boomed on amidst its dust and glitter, its glamor and vice, its honky-tonks and its grand opera. Bone-hungry emigrants huddled in its streets; millionaire investors bought and sold by the book while champagne bubbled at the club. Handsome, porticoed mansions went up on the east side while the west side sprawled lewdly among its fifty bars and brothels.

"Hell-on-Horseback," Jean Markle called the place, and Cheyenne took no offense. The soiled half was too jaded to care and the other half too busy with its boom. For in this fall of the year 1883 a quarter million cattle changed hands, at club, bank and bar, with most of them never being actually counted. The thing to watch was not roundups but soaring prices. Big owners, instead of riding the range, preferred to ride leather chairs at the Cheyenne Club on whose wall was always posted latest quotations from the Chicago Livestock Exchange.

They watched three-cent steers go to four cents on the hoof; four-cent beef go to a nickel; five-cent grassers jump to six. Think of it! Sixty dollars for a thousand-pound grasser! And you didn't even need to own the grass. It was free grass and all you needed to do was buy a herd you'd never seen, trusting a book tally which said it was still grazing somewhere on the wide ranges of Wyoming. No wonder it was full steam ahead and damn the blizzards! What with investors swarming from Europe and the east, bidding eagerly to get in on the ground floor! No wonder the Apperson Brothers, from Philadelphia, spent much more time asking if a fall-fat Wyoming steer was a bargain at thirty dollars, than they did in inspecting the actual visible assets of Wally Grimes.

Here and there a few cautious voices gave warning—but the roar of the boom drowned them out. Colonel Luke Murrin looked sadly down his bar as cowmen customers talked exultantly of six-cent beef. "They're not worth it, gentlemen!" he warned in his soft, genteel voice. "They'll drop to five, four, even three cents before we're a year older. You ought to be selling, not buying."

They laughed at him. But Luke Murrin kept at them. He stood there toying with his gold watch chain and warned solemnly: "Take my advice, gentlemen. If you have steers to shed, prepare to shed them now!"

Yet the spiral of speculation went on.

Fifty miles to the northwest a buckskin gelding grazed the swales of upper Sybille. Hidden in its mane was a note which, if found and delivered, would prick and explode the beef boom like a pin in a bubble. It would set Wyoming by the ears. It would throw the WSGA into panic. It would frighten and scatter investors. Checkbooks would snap shut and prices would fall like lead in a vacuum. For if *one* book-counter was a knave, instead of only a foolhardy optimist, maybe there were others. The scandal would flash to New York, London, Edinburgh, where men would think twice before buying sheer figures, instead of hair and flesh and horns tallied on the hoof.

Riders of District Number One's roundup came up Sybille, saw the buckskin grazing there and passed it by. This was a roundup of cattle, not of horses. While down at Cheyenne Wally Grimes planned his final date with the Apperson boys. He'd take them to dinner at the club and make sure Gerry Lorton was right across the table. Gerry would talk not to the Appersons but to the table in general—about what a fool he'd been to sell the Boxed M, now that steers were six cents and still going up. It wouldn't take any urging. The Appersons were ready for the kill, and their check was good at any bank.

At Clem Harwood's cabin near the fairgrounds, two young women tied their buggy and went in. "We got a copy of the telegram, Uncle Clem." Gail Garrison held out a scrap of paper.

"'Meet me in Morton's Pass noon tomorrow. Skeets,'" Harwood read aloud. He looked quizzically from Gail to Jean Markle. "Well, what's wrong with that?"

"Nothing," Gail said, "if Skeets really sent the message. But suppose he didn't! Suppose someone else signed Skeets' name!"

Harwood cocked an eye. "What makes you think it wasn't Skeets?"

Gail hesitated. She wasn't ready to talk about Gerald Lorton. Really there was nothing to say about him except that he'd taken a train trip to Laramie. And why shouldn't he? As a broker handling stocks in a dozen cattle corporations, he might have a customer in Laramie. It wouldn't be fair to mention Gerry.

But she could mention Grimes. "I just think we ought to find out about it, Uncle Clem. We know someone tried to kill Russ Hyatt at least three times. Once they hauled him away in Grimes' wagon. The same Grimes who came to the jail and got him out! Why?"

Clem scratched his chin, nodding shrewdly. "Grimes is mixed up in it, some way," he reasoned. "Could be he forged a message and had it sent from Laramie. After posting a killer in Morton's Pass!"

"*I* think," Jean Markle said in her clear, frank voice, "that we should tell the sheriff and let *him* handle it."

"Russ wouldn't want us to," Harwood brooded. "Remember what he said. A pard of his is in a fix. This pard's a goner if we start stirrin' up sheriffs. Reckon that's why Russ didn't go to the law himself."

Gail looked at him helplessly. "But if the telegram is a decoy, we can't just fold our hands and do nothing."

"We don't need to." Clem Harwood stood up and looked at his watch. "I'll ketch the next train to Laramie. I can make the operator there describe the man who filed the message. If he wasn't a lanky, sandy-faced cowboy he wasn't Skeets. If he wasn't Skeets I'll hire me a horse and take a ride. I'll ride thirty mile north to Morton's Pass and see if any dirt's been done there."

Gail spent a troubled night, wondering what Uncle Clem would learn at Laramie. Gerald Lorton was back in town and he'd sent a note over asking her to supper at the club. She'd sent back word she had a headache and couldn't go. She didn't want to see Gerry again until she heard from Uncle Clem. If the sender of the message was described as a tall, light-haired man in a tailor-made suit he couldn't be Skeets Carson. And he was sure to be Gerald Lorton.

The first train Uncle Clem could get back on was Number 2, due at 11:30 in the morning. Well before that hour Gail drove down to the Inter-

Ocean and picked up Jean. The two girls were waiting on the depot platform when Number 2 pulled in from the west. Passengers got off, but Clem Harwood wasn't among them.

A sick feeling came over Gail. Her eyes met Jean's and the eastern girl said, "So Skeets didn't send it!"

It looked that way. Otherwise Uncle Clem would have caught the first train back to Cheyenne. Gail saw a sack thrown off the mail car. It gave her a thought. "Let's go to the post office, Jean."

They drove up Ferguson and tied at the post office. Inside, Gail found a clerk she knew. She was expecting a letter on the morning train. It might be addressed to her house. "But let me have it right here, please."

They waited while the mail was sorted. "Here you are, Miss Garrison." The clerk gave her a letter postmarked Laramie.

Gail read it with Jean looking over her shoulder.

> Dear Gail:
>
> Operator says small boy brought message. Man handed boy a four-bit telegram and a dollar, told him to take it to the depot and keep the change. Operator didn't ask boy what man looked like. Can't locate boy. Might be any street kid, or a kid from some emigrant wagon

passing through. Skeets wouldn't sneak a message over that way. So it was rigged. By Wally Grimes, likely. I'm riding for Morton's Pass. Let you know what I find there.

CLEM.

"He'll find Russ dead!" Gail predicted hopelessly. "Russ and Skeets too."

Jean patted her shoulder. "Let's don't give up like that. Hyatt looks like he can take care of himself. I'll bet Skeets can too. Anyway all we can do now is wait for Uncle Clem to get back."

Gail dropped Jean at the hotel and drove home. After that she kept out of sight to avoid Gerry Lorton. She didn't want to see him—not till she was sure. Someone had rigged that message, but she still couldn't make herself believe it was Lorton. It could be some Boxed M rider or anyone else in the pay of Grimes.

It was fairly clear now that Russ had confided in Skeets. He'd convalesced at the TOT bunkhouse with Skeets looking after him. Probably Russ had sent Skeets on a scouting expedition to look for the "pard in a fix."

When she admitted that much Gail also had to admit that Skeets himself was now in the same "fix." Otherwise the Grimes gang wouldn't know enough to use his name as a decoy.

Again Gail spent a restless night. And again, at

11:30 in the morning, she and Jean Markle were at the depot to meet Number 2.

Clem Harwood didn't arrive on it. This time Gail hardly expected him. A round-trip horseback ride between Laramie and Morton's Pass would take two days—one up and one back. "We're a day early, Jean. Let's meet this same train tomorrow."

Two hours before Number 2 was due a morning later, Clem Harwood arrived in the caboose of a freight. He looked old and tired and grim as he got into a hack at the depot. "Carey Block," he said.

As the hack rattled up Ferguson, Harwood wondered if he was doing right. He'd decided to have it out with Grimes. Actually the trip to Laramie had netted him not one scrap of proof against Grimes. All he knew was that someone else than Skeets had filed the telegram. He'd found no sign of a fight at Morton's Pass. Nothing to show that Russ Hyatt had been there.

Just the same it was time to face Grimes. In the caboose coming down Sherman Hill Clem Harwood had brooded over it and had decided to make Grimes explain the buckboard. And what about a man named Alford? The Boxed M did much of its trading at Laramie and so Harwood had asked about the crew there. "They took on a new outfit in July," a Laramie liveryman said. "Some of 'em come from Arizony." Asked for names the liveryman only remembered one. Alford.

It was through Alford's transom, Harwood remembered, that a man named Judnick had shot at Russ Hyatt. There'd been a third man in the room. Grimes? Yes, it was time to look Grimes in the eye and ask questions.

The hack stopped at the Carey Block. Harwood told the driver to wait. Then he went up to Grimes' office on the second floor.

Its door wasn't locked. Harwood went in and found the office empty. The roll-top desk was open and papers were scattered about. So Grimes had probably stepped out to be gone only a few minutes. Maybe to the bank downstairs or across to the post office.

The white-haired freighter sat down to wait. Waiting, he took a look at the scattered papers in case they might tell him something he didn't already know about Grimes. They didn't.

He opened a desk drawer and glanced through odds and ends there. The drawer had a .38 gun but it wasn't loaded. Harwood looked in desk pigeonholes and in one of them he found a book of check stubs. The last check in it had been written less than a week ago. The amount on the stub was three hundred dollars. Drawn to the order of cash at the First National Bank. The date was the one on which Hyatt had killed Idaho Brown in a gunfight.

Three hundred dollars! The figure tugged at a corner of Harwood's mind, teasing him, and then he remembered. Exactly that sum was found in the dead man's pocket.

Just a happenso, maybe. And maybe not! It could be murder money. Killers have to be paid, generally with cash in advance. Anyway it made one more question—and a hot one—to ask Grimes.

15

At the alley gate of a corral back of the Bon Ton livery, on Eddy Street just below Nineteenth, two dusty riders waited for Grimes. They'd ridden in from Morton's Pass, stopping at the Boxed M to pack their kits and pick up fresh horses.

For these two had had enough. They were leaving this range for good—just the minute they collected from Grimes. "Only we don't tell Wally that," Alford said slyly. "If he knows we're diggin' out he won't pay us off."

Spoffard pulled his hatbrim lower, sucked at his cigaret. He'd skidded a long way these last seven years. The swagger of his heyday, when he'd been a tramp-killing marshal in Kansas, was all gone. "We'd be suckers to stay," he agreed, "after lettin' Hyatt get through us. He'll head fer a sheriff, one of these days. When he does you an' me'd better be a long piece off."

Alford looked half a block north to a telegraph pole at Nineteenth and Eddy. "I was right here when they strung up Mosier, Spoff. I'll never forget the way he kicked, hangin' there."

"None of that fer me, Alf." Spoffard's grin was pale. "And it could happen easy enough now, after we fluked on gettin' Hyatt. I don't mind risks long as I got a few cards. But . . . Sh! Here comes Wally."

Grimes, crossing from the Carey Block to the post office, had seen them canter up to the bank hitchrack. But he didn't want them going up to his office. Nor could he risk talking to them on a crowded sidewalk, right by the Stockgrowers' National. So a quick head-signal had sent them a few blocks away to a spot where they'd reported to him before. The alley gate back of the Bon Ton livery.

They'd ridden in, he supposed, to report on the Morton's Pass ambush. Grimes joined them, nervous and eager. "What happened?"

"We got him," Spoffard said. He looked both ways, then twisted his mouth to speak lower. "He put up a fight and we lost Jud. And Sid got nicked a little. But we got Hyatt. We buried him right next to Judnick."

Sweat of relief moistened the loose, fleshy face of Grimes. "You wouldn't lie to me? You got any proof?"

"Sure we have," Alford said. "Clawin' ca'tridges from his pocket he dropped this. Take a look." What he showed Grimes was a receipt made out to Russell Hyatt for the last room he'd rented at the Inter-Ocean Hotel. They'd found it on the pass butte while cleaning up empty shells Hyatt had strewn there.

The relief grew in Grimes' eyes and the look of doubt disappeared. The receipt convinced him. It was dated the day Hyatt had received the telegram at the hotel. Alford couldn't have it unless he'd tangled with Hyatt since that day. Grimes gave a sallow smile. "I feel better now."

"So'll we," Spoffard said, "soon as you pay us off. Five hun'erd cash apiece, you said."

"Wait till I . . ."

"We'll take it right now," Alford cut in, holding out his hand. "It was worth twice that, gettin' Hyatt off your neck."

"Come across," Spoffard snapped. Neither of them believed the Grimes cattle deal would ever go through, now that Hyatt survived to tell about it. And when it blew up, there wouldn't be any payoff at all. A thousand wasn't much, but it was enough to take them a long way from Cheyenne.

"We're stickin' right with you, Wally," Alford insisted, "till you settle up."

It left Grimes no choice. After all they'd earned the money. And Judnick getting killed meant a saving of five hundred. He gave cautious glances to right and left, then brought out his wallet. "Here you are. Now make yourselves scarce till I need you."

"Sure thing, Wally." As he took the money Spoffard drooped an eyelid in a covert wink at Alford. A minute later they were asaddle, riding fast and forever out of the affairs of Wally Grimes.

Grimes hurried toward the Carey Block and on the way stopped in at the Cheyenne *Leader.*

There he paid for a classified ad to run daily for a week.

> LOST: pair of silver spurs and belt buckle with monogram G. Finder return to W. Grimes, Carey Block, and receive small reward.

Nothing incriminating about it, because once Grimes actually *had* lost a pair of spurs and a buckle. But to Sid and Jonas it would be a signal. Westbound trains carried the *Leader* to every station on the line and a few copies were dropped off daily at Medicine Bow. As often as possible Jonas rode to the Bow to pick up a paper. The ad would tell them Hyatt was dead and to dispose of the hostages at once.

Grimes went on to the Carey Block and up to his office. Opening the door he found a veteran freighter named Harwood sitting there, thin-lipped and grim, shaggy white hair hanging to his shoulders and his eyes full of questions.

"I been waitin' for yuh." The words were short-clipped and the steady gaze brought the sweat of fear to Grimes' face. He closed the door, went to his swivel chair at the desk. "Waiting for me? What for?"

"To ask you four riddles," Harwood said.

"What riddles?"

"Number one." Harwood tossed him a book

of check stubs. "Take a look at the last stub. An even three hundred dollars. How did you spend it?"

Grimes tightened a little but recovered quickly. "Can't see it's any of your business. Paying bills here and there, I suppose. I don't keep tabs on my pocket money."

"Number two. Who signed Skeets' name to a telegram?"

"First I ever heard of it." Grimes had a grip on himself now and his answer came truculently. This old man was bluffing, shooting in the dark without any real proof.

"Number three. When Judnick shot through Alford's transom, were you there?"

Grimes licked a tongue around his lips. "You're crazy! Of course I wasn't there."

"Last, what about a Boxed M buckboard taken out of the Bon Ton barn the evening someone tied Russ Hyatt with a pair of my boot laces? Supplies for the ranch, I suppose?"

"Sure. Couple of my men were in for supplies that day."

"And drove home at night? Which way did they go? I'm a freighter and I know every wagon trail in Wyoming."

"I didn't ask which way." Grimes was cautious, feeling for every word.

"Then you'd better find out fast," Harwood said, "and dig me up a satisfactory answer.

Because the direct, honest route to the Boxed M is right through Fort Russell and on up Crow Creek past the TOT. A longer and rougher way to go is up Pole Creek where they found Hyatt. Prove to me your buckboard went up Crow Creek, and you're off the hook."

"Of course it went up Crow Creek," Grimes said. "It's ten miles shorter that way."

"If it went up Crow Creek it was seen. A sentry at the fort challenged it and let it pass. Three-four hundred soldiers saw it pass by the barracks. Hands at the TOT saw it go by. They'd see it at old man Jimson's place further up the Crow. Somebody said howdy to that buckboard if it went the short, honest trail to Mesa Mountain."

"No doubt they did," Grimes agreed with a shrug. "So what? I wasn't along myself. You can't expect me to know every time one of my hands says howdy on the road."

"The driver was named Alford," Harwood said. "The Bon Ton tells me it was Alford who called for the rig. He's in town right now. Little while ago I saw him ride past this office window." Harwood looked at his watch. "It's ten o'clock. I'll give you till noon, Grimes. You know where I live. If you're not there by noon, with the right answer, I'll take it up with the sheriff."

Grimes fished for words but none of them fit. His face was damp and gleaming as the freighter moved to the door. In the doorway Harwood turned with a final word. "Just bring me the name of *one* witness who saw the buckboard on an honest road, and we'll forget the whole thing. Be there by noon, Grimes."

Grimes heard his boots thump down the stairs. Looking out he saw Harwood get into a waiting hack and drive off.

Bitterly he damned Harwood. Why did he have to poke his nose into it just as all the other hazards were cleared away? Hyatt was dead. Cortney and Skeets would never be heard from. Only those three could have told tales on Grimes.

Yet Clem Harwood had made a shrewd guess or two. Not about Cortney. Cortney hadn't even been missed. The guesses were about a telegram and a buckboard. Harwood couldn't prove a thing. But still he could make trouble. He could stir up the law and the newspapers. If he did that, good-bye Appersons. Any breath of suspicion against Grimes would scare them off.

All his smooth planning would go by the boards. Except for Clem Harwood there wasn't an eyebrow being lifted. If he could only keep it that way for another two weeks! By then he'd be in Chicago cashing Apperson's sight draft. He'd be in the clear, moving fast, let the fall roundup tally show what it would.

As Grimes sank into his desk chair, he abused himself for dismissing Alford and Spoffard. He'd told them to make themselves scarce till he needed them. Now he needed them—desperately! Needed them to deal with Clem Harwood. But they'd left town. Two hours was all Harwood gave him. Two hours to come up with a witness who'd seen the buckboard pass up the Crow Creek road. He tried to think of someone he could bribe. Someone who for fifty dollars would swear he'd seen the buckboard.

Would it satisfy Harwood? A reputable witness would. But not some bar bum, or some pick-up gunman like Idaho Brown. It would take straight talking to satisfy Harwood. What *he* needs, Grimes thought savagely, is a bullet. If he could only get hold of Spoff! Or Alf! For an extra thousand either of them would pay a quick call at Harwood's cabin.

But they were gone from Cheyenne.

Grimes opened a desk drawer and saw a .38 gun. Could he do it himself? Did he have the guts? He took the gun out, fingered it fearfully. He wasn't a gunman. It was easier to hire gunmen than to take a risk oneself.

Clem Harwood lived alone out there. He wouldn't expect Grimes to come with a gun. Nearest house was two blocks away and nobody'd hear a shot. Wally Grimes sat there sweating, balancing risk against risk as he loaded the .38 gun.

Gail and Jean got to the depot just before train time. The board said Number 2 was half an hour late. That would put it in at noon. "Gives me time to file my copy," Jean said. "I was up half the night writing it."

"I was afraid of that," Gail said. There were tired lines under Jean's eyes.

After filing her copy the New York girl rejoined Gail on the platform. "You're working too hard, Jean. What you need is some fun. A romance or two at the club."

Jean's laugh was at her own expense. "I've already had one," she confessed. "At least I was beginning to think so. Then he went off on an elk hunt." Jean made her lips droop ruefully. "And without even saying good-bye."

"Where did you meet him?"

"There was an officers' ball at the fort. We were both strangers. I'd just arrived from New York and he from Boston. So he danced with me four times."

"Did you see him again?"

"Twice. Once we went to the Opera House to hear Will Carleton read from his 'Farm Ballads.' We laughed and cried when he did pieces like 'Betsy and I Are Out' and 'Over the Hill to the Poorhouse.' Then he took me to dinner at the club."

"And then?"

"Then, alas, he walked out of my life. Just as I was thinking I'd made an impression!"

Behind Jean Markle's light tone Gail suspected

a hurt and so she quickly changed the subject. "What was this latest copy of yours about, Jean? More about the sins of Cheyenne?"

Instantly Jean was serious and again the militant crusader. "The worst scandal of all, really. Election frauds. You Wyoming women should be ashamed, Gail! You're the only women who can vote. And look what happens!"

"Don't blame me! I won't be old enough to vote for a month yet." Then Gail added curiously, "Just what *does* happen?"

"I've gone over the records. The respectable women don't vote at all. The vice-house women vote many times. Repeating is easy because you don't have to register in Wyoming. You just walk up to a polling place and a man asks your name. You say John Smith or Jane Doe. He writes it in a book and hands you a ballot. You vote, then go to the next precinct and call yourself Jane Brown. And you vote again."

Gail was shocked. "Are you sure?"

"Both your local papers admit it. At the last election, the advance agent of a show troupe voted seven times. Emigrants passing through town often vote. It's like market-day bargaining. This house of ill fame is sold by its madam to a candidate for a lump sum; that laboring man's lodging house fetches so much per head. Carriages roll through the streets carrying loafers, tramps, cutthroats and harpies to the polls, while wives and daughters of the WSGA stay home."

Gail stared. "And you sent that to New York?"

"That and a lot more. It will all be in the *Globe-Sun*, next Sunday." The shocked look on Gail's face made Jean's relax. "Forgive me, Gail. There I go waving my torch again. Isn't that our train?"

Number 2 pulled in from the west. Many people got off but Gail failed to see Clem Harwood.

"Were you expecting someone, Miss Garrison?"

A brakeman touched his cap to Gail. She'd often ridden on this train because the nearest rail point to the Cross D was Rawlins, a six-hour run west of here. All trainmen knew the Garrison family by sight.

"I thought maybe Uncle Clem Harwood might come in," Gail said. "Do you know him?"

"Sure I do," the brakeman said. "Used to be your dad's wagon boss, didn't he? But hold on! At Laramie the agent said Clem Harwood caught a freight right ahead of us. Rode a caboose over the hill."

"So *that's* why we missed him! He's already here and we didn't know it. Come on, Jean."

Gail smiled her thanks to the brakeman and hurried Jean to the buggy. In a minute they were driving toward the fairgrounds.

As they passed the Cheyenne Club Gail asked: "You haven't seen him since he had you to dinner here? Your Mr. . . . ?"

"Cortney," Jean supplied. "Miles Cortney."

Gail turned north up Dodge Street. They passed Twentieth and the last house. The last house, that is, except a stout log cabin two blocks ahead. No horse was tied in front of it. But Uncle Clem, Gail reasoned, would have come from the freight yards in a hack.

She drew up in front of the cabin and they got out. "Uncle Clem!" Gail called, knocking. There was no answer.

"He hasn't come home yet," Jean concluded.

Yet a window was open and the door stood slightly ajar. "*Someone's* home," Gail said. "Uncle Clem!" she called again.

Again no answer. "Maybe he's asleep," Jean suggested.

"I'll peek and see." Gail pushed the door open and looked in.

"Uncle Clem!" This time it was a half-smothered cry of horror as both girls froze in the doorway. Clem Harwood lay on the cabin floor, his eyes glazed and his head bloody.

Jean Markle came out of it first. She'd had stern practice, these last few weeks, at facing facts and the seamy side of Cheyenne. She went in and kneeled beside Clem Harwood. When she turned, her face had a marble paleness. "He's been shot, Gail. And he's . . . dead!"

16

Keeping screened by the brush, Russ Hyatt slipped quietly down-creek. He'd made camp in an aspen copse half a mile below the sheds. As he changed the picketing of his horse he remembered it belonged to Judnick. So it must have been here before. It might whinny at sight or sound of other horses, hoping to be stalled in a shed up there. To play safe, Russ moved the horse a little way up a ravine.

He made coffee and ate the last of Judnick's bacon. Then he circled afoot to a high point from which he could look down on the hideout. Lazy smoke drifted from the cabin chimney. No men were in sight but the corral showed seven horses and a mule.

Russ frowned. If each horse meant an outlaw the odds against him were too long. He considered riding south to Medicine Bow, or north to the Platte Valley, for a crew of cowboys to raid this place. But they'd be noisy about it and the men in the cabin would kill the two prisoners. Or it might happen while Russ was gone. Any minute their death warrant could come from Grimes at Cheyenne.

Only five saddles were in sight, so Russ concluded that two of the seven horses were the buckboard team. He could see the buckboard by a shed. Of the five saddle horses, one was Skeets Carson's and another was a blue roan which Russ himself had stabled in the IXL livery at Cheyenne.

So the odds, after all, were only three to one and Russ decided against riding for help. He'd shoot it out with them himself, come nightfall.

A little before sundown Jonas came out with a bucket. It would be so easy for Russ to pick him off with his rifle! But two other outlaws were inside and they'd take it out on his friends.

It must be a complete, sudden surprise with all three of the enemy bunched. Like at supper. A man with a knife and fork in his hands and with his knees under a table can't pull a gun very fast.

Jonas took a bucket of water from the creek and carried it inside. Then Sid came out for firewood. Russ hadn't glimpsed the third man yet.

He was beginning to hope there was no third man when he heard boots on gravel. Someone was coming down the opposite hillside. He was a short, hairy man wearing a duckbill cap. In one hand he had a rifle and in the other a broadpawed snowshoe rabbit.

Russ felt like kicking himself. First for not tying into the other two before this one came home. Second for almost giving himself away by camping down-creek. Had the man hunted in that direction he'd have stumbled on a saddle and a picketed horse.

Jonas appeared in the cabin doorway. "That all you got, Fritz? I was set fer grouse."

"I'll getcha some grouse tomorrow," Fritz promised. He went on to the creek, skinned and dressed his kill, then took it to the cabin.

The sun dropped below a piney skyline and light faded. Russ had them all spotted now. So he circled back to his camp and from there moved upcreek through the brush. He stopped back of the main shed.

From the looks of it, the cabin had one large square room and a small lean-to. The big room had a door and two windows; the lean-to had no opening at all. Just a storage space, probably. The prisoners could be in it; or they could be in a cellar under the floor.

Dusk deepened and a light came on in the cabin. Not a candle but a kerosene lamp. The window on this side had no curtain. Through it Russ could see the inmates move around. They were on their feet, so they weren't eating yet.

To be out of line from a window Russ moved a little way up the brush. From there he stepped out and advanced warily toward the cabin's lean-to side. The rifle was in his left hand, a six-gun in his right. His boot kicked a pebble and he stood still for a moment, holding his breath. If they came at him he'd drop the six-gun and use the rifle.

No one came out. Back of him he heard horses stir in the corral. Far up the slope of Warbonnet an elk bugled. Russ advanced another twenty steps and flattened himself against the rear wall of the lean-to. He could feel his heart thumping. Were Cort and Skeets just beyond this wall? For long minutes he waited there while dusk dissolved into dark.

He wouldn't need the rifle now. For fast, close-up shooting the short gun would serve him better. He leaned the rifle against the cabin wall. Then he slid quietly along the wall to the corner. Around it he saw a board porch, about a foot higher than the ground.

A window was between him and the porch. By stooping low, Russ passed under it. Stepping up on the porch he creaked a board. Full night had come now. Dark would be at his back when he opened the door. The forty-five was in his right hand, cocked. Voices came from inside. A bench scraped as it was pulled up to a table. A tone of disgust marked Sid's voice. "A measly rabbit! And the whole woods fulla grouse!"

Forks scraped on plates. And Fritz retorted nasally: "I didn't come home empty-handed. Which is more'n you can say, Sid. Howcome you let that guy get away?"

Sid offered no excuse. And Jonas said: "Makes

good gravy, anyway. Let's have some coffee, Fritz."

Now was the time, with Fritz pouring coffee!

Russ kicked the door open and stepped in with a level gun. He waved it in a short arc. "It's my drop," he said.

Two, on this side of the table, had their backs to Russ. Jonas sat across from them and was facing the door. Fritz dropped the coffeepot and twisted around. Sid half turned with his hands raising shakily upward. And Jonas dropped out of sight under the table.

Russ had expected a go for guns by all three and now he could only see two, Sid with his hands ear-high, Fritz twisted awkwardly with his legs pointing one way while facing the other. "What the hell . . . ?"

"Freeze!" Russ said. His aim covered Fritz but was ready to swing on Sid. What bothered him was not being able to see Jonas. Only Sid had his hands up and Russ had to keep his eyes level. He didn't dare look down to see which end of the table, if any, Jonas would crawl out from under.

And unless someone drew on him, Russ couldn't make himself shoot. He'd grown up under a code which banned shooting till the other side went for its guns. Damn them! Why didn't they? Sid seemed scared stiff. But a scared man is dangerous. Fritz merely stared, mouth open, his knees still under the table while his round, hairy face was toward Russ.

He was so close that Russ could have punched the gun into his mouth. For an age-long ten seconds the stalemate lasted. All through it Russ kept a cocked-gun aim on Fritz while Sid held his hands ear-high. Beyond them, hanging on a peg, he saw a hat. A cowman's hat, new, high-crowned and fawn-colored—a headgear once worn by Miles Cortney of Boston.

Then a voice from the lean-to. "Is that you, Russ?"

It was the voice of Skeets Carson and it snapped the tension. Nerves cracked. Suddenly one of Sid's hands dropped to his holster as Fritz did the same. Both made fast draws and Russ pulled his own trigger twice. The range was point-blank and he couldn't miss, even though he had to shift aim between shots.

He saw them go down and then his hat bounced. It was Jonas shooting from the floor. Jonas had his head out from under the table and only the awkwardness of his stance saved Russ. The man was on knees and one hand, his gun in the other. His second bullet singed Russ. The man was almost underfoot and Russ kicked at his gun. Someone else was shooting and Russ couldn't understand why he didn't get hit. "Burn 'em down, Russ!" Skeets yelled from the lean-to.

Sid had fallen sidewise, his gun bumping the

floor. And Fritz lay on his back with a bullet-cut throat. But a gun was still in his hand and he was shooting with it. Shooting wildly and blindly as he died there. One of his shots hit a fawn-colored hat and it fell from its peg. Jonas was the only one to worry about and Russ kicked again at the man's gun, sent it flying across the room.

"Whang into 'em, cowboy!" Skeets cheered from beyond the lean-to door. And Russ, covering Jonas, stooped to take a gun from Fritz.

But Fritz, dying, got in one more convulsive, unaimed shot. His gun arm was outflung on the floor and his last trigger squeeze swept the floor with a bullet. Jonas, on hands and knees not three feet away, took it in the head. He flattened quietly and the room was still, smoke-choked. A smell of burnt powder filled it. Russ could hardly believe that he himself had fired only twice.

Twice at point-blank range. Yet when he looked down he saw three dead men on the floor. It was Fritz who'd done for Jonas. Russ stood with his pulses pounding through another age-long ten seconds and then out of the stillness came words from Skeets. Fearful words, this time, shot with a dreadful suspense. "Did they get you, Russ?"

Russ picked up the three guns. Then he looked at the lean-to door and saw a padlock on it. "Where do they keep the key, Skeets?" he asked, his voice jaded and hollow.

"You hear that, Mr. Cortney? The old son-of-a-gun!" Skeets was cheering again. "Wants to know where they keep the key! How would I know, you old gun-fanning buzzard? Look in their pants and get us to hell outa here."

The tightness left Hyatt's face and a tired smile took its place. Jonas ought to have the key, because for part of the day he'd been here alone. Russ found it in his jacket pocket and unlocked the lean-to door.

Skeets Carson bounced out, slapping Russ on the shoulder. "You old son-of-a-gun! We'd about give you up." He looked underfed and his unshaven face showed bruises. Cortney lay on a blanket back of him. No words came from him but Russ saw him raise a hand weakly in salute.

Skeets looked at the dead men, then out through the open front door. "Where's the sheriffs, Russ?"

"Nearest one's at Laramie," Russ said. "There's another at Rawlins and another at Cheyenne. Which county are we in, anyway?"

Skeets gaped. "No sheriffs? You mean you done it all by yourself?"

Russ took an oil lamp into the lean-to. Cortney looked up at him, hollow-eyed and gaunt, the bones of his face showing. There was a half-healed gash on his head. "How's the elk huntin', Cort?" Russ asked it lightly, sensing that the man's spirits were even sicker than his body.

Cortney's smile had gameness and his lips made one faint word. "Thanks."

"He needs nourishment, Russ. Let's start him off with a shot of this." Skeets had found a pint of brandy and poured a stiff dram of it.

"It's too much for an empty stomach," Russ said. "Drink half of it yourself."

"Since you insist!" Skeets grinned and downed half the liquor. They made Cortney sit up and held the rest of it to his lips. "Jonas clubbed him down one day," Skeets explained as Russ looked at the gash on Cortney's head, "to keep him quiet while a couple of roundup hands rode by. That was before I got here. Right now I better dish up some grub."

An hour later Russ and Skeets sat full-fed at the table. The room had three bunks and Cortney was resting in one of them. They hadn't needed to cook supper since it had already been prepared by Sid and Jonas. Russ looked at Cortney and saw that he was relaxed, some of the haggardness already gone. "That's mostly what he needs," Skeets said. "Nourishment and a little pamperin'. That ride in a buckboard chounced him around some. Him all tied up like a pig-stringed calf. It sure didn't do him any good."

"How did they grab you, Skeets?"

"I found their sign and followed too close. They made three night stops on the way here. One night while I was asleep they doubled back on me. Woke up with a gun ticklin' my chin."

Russ moved to a window, his eyes searching the dark out there. "One of us better stay awake, Skeets, so it won't happen again. I mean in case Grimes sends a messenger here."

"Nobody he can send," Skeets countered. "You say Spoff and Alf headed back toward Cheyenne. They couldn't make it there and then get back here for another day or two yet. And Shorty's with the roundup on Chugwater."

"Shorty? Who's he?"

"Far as I can tell he's the only one you haven't met up with. Jonas and Fritz talked free and easy right in front of us—they figgered we wouldn't ever leave here alive. So I heard all about the Boxed M setup. Main crew's on the level. To get 'em out of the way while Grimes cooks up this long tally sale, he sent 'em out on fall roundup. Rest are gunnies he brought up from the Mexico border. He kept these border guys at the Boxed M, in case he needed 'em for gun work, and in case a prospect came out to look the ranch over. All but one. A jigger named Shorty. He had Shorty join the roundup as Boxed M tallyman."

Russ nodded shrewdly. "Played it cute, didn't he? If a buyer went to the roundup for a look at the tally, he could be lied to by Shorty. If he went to the ranch, he could be lied to by Spoffard. Or even if he talked to honest Boxed M hands at the roundup, they couldn't tell him much. They were all taken on since the spring tally and the fall tally's not finished yet."

"In a nutshell," Skeets agreed.

"Did they talk about a man named Lou?"

"Once or twice. Nothin' you could pin a tag on. Seems like he ramrodded this whole play. Some smart guy who stays mostly in Cheyenne."

"Did they mention the name Lorton? Gerry Lorton?"

"Not in front of us, they didn't."

Russ dragged on his cigaret. "This is Albany County, isn't it?"

"Yeh, but not far from the Carbon County line."

"Okay, Skeets. We got to do two things fast. First, tell the law at Cheyenne all about Grimes. That way they can stop him from sawing off his long tally on somebody. Next, we got to deliver three dead men to the coroner at Laramie."

Skeets nodded, glancing toward the lean-to door behind which the dead men lay under canvas. They'd been killed in a county of which Laramie was the seat. "But the nearest rail point," Russ added, "is Medicine Bow. Cort and I'll catch a train for Cheyenne at the Bow. It's the quickest way to get there. We've got to make sure Grimes doesn't get the wind up and take off. About fifty-five miles from here to the Bow."

"That's a long ride for Cort," Skeets brooded, "the shape he's in."

Cortney heard and spoke from the bunk. "I can make it all right."

"We'll take two days for it," Russ decided.

"I'll heat up a tub of water, Mr. Cortney," Skeets said. "A bath and a shave won't hurt us any."

After a night's sleep and a generous breakfast a little of his old color came back to Miles Cortney. He picked up his high-crowned cattleman's hat and looked at bullet holes through it. Then with a grin he cocked it at a proud angle on his head. "A girl I met in Cheyenne," he said, "helped me pick out this hat. Wait till she sees me in it now!"

Russ didn't ask who the girl was.

When they pulled out of French Creek Skeets drove the buckboard with Cortney seated by him. The dead men lay under a tarp in the wagon bed and two saddlehorses were tied to the endgate. Russ rode his own blue roan. All other stock, including the pack mule, was set free on the range.

At La Prele Creek they turned up-canyon. A three-hour climb took them to the top of Cold Springs Pass, treeless on its southern side. From it they could see far south across the Laramie Plains. This pass was about twenty miles west of the stage road through Downey Park.

They moved slowly down the slope, brakes on. "What d'yuh reckon they'll do with that guy?" Skeets wondered. "Grimes, I mean."

"He'll go to the pen," Russ said. "That's for sure. Betcha the WSGA'd see him hanged, if they could."

"Why can't they?"

"Because as far as we know he hasn't murdered anybody. He tried to, but it didn't come off."

Skeets gave a wry grin. "He didn't miss it far. I was scared stiff every time Jonas came back from the Bow with a late copy of the *Leader*. They always looked for an ad in it. About lost silver spurs. It'd tip 'em off you'd been taken care of. Then they could take care of us. Like this." Skeets sawed an edge of his hand across his throat.

They got down to the flat country and there made better time. Antelope bounded across the trail. By sundown they made the little Medicine River which snaked its treeless way across the plain. In camp there Cortney again got a sound sleep. "You can stop babying me now," he said in the morning.

"Can you sit a saddle?"

"Don't worry about that." Again the Boston man cocked a bullet-punctured hat proudly on his head.

"Then here's where we split." Russ pointed toward a fork in the trail just ahead. "Skeets, you take the left fork and drive the buckboard to Laramie. Turn your load over to county officers there. Tell them not to let anything leak out till I've reported to Cheyenne. Cort and I'll take the right fork to the Bow. We'll leave our horses there and hop a train to Cheyenne."

The twenty-mile saddle ride tired Cortney but they made it well before time for Number 4, due through eastbound at four in the afternoon.

"*You'll* have to buy the tickets," Cortney said. "Alford and Judnick took every cent I had."

"How much was that?" Russ asked.

"My wallet had eighty dollars. That's all they found on me till the second night out. Then Judnick worked me over again and slit open my belt. It was a secret money belt with ten one-hundred-dollar bills in it. I've carried it for years in case I got stranded somewhere."

"They cleaned me out too, Cort." But since then Russ had been in Cheyenne and had dipped into his savings. He was buying tickets when Number 3, westbound and several hours late, puffed to a stop at the Medicine Bow depot.

Chicago, Omaha and Cheyenne papers were tossed off. "Let's see if Grimes has unloaded yet," Russ said, standing by while a bundle of *Leaders* was being untied. Any big cattle deal was always headline news in Cheyenne. And Grimes was sure to be working fast. "If he's put that long tally deal over, I'm not going to be any too popular in cow circles. I mean for not tellin' on him while I had the chance."

But when he spread out the latest issue of the Cheyenne *Leader*, the headlines were exactly the reverse of what he'd feared.

POPULAR FREIGHTER MURDERED
CLEM HARWOOD SHOT DEAD BY MYSTERY CALLER

WALLY GRIMES UNDER SUSPICION
BOXED M OWNER HELD PENDING SEARCH FOR MISSING WITNESS, RUSS HYATT

Russ read half a column and let Cortney read the rest. Then he filed a wire to the Cheyenne sheriff. "Will arrive Cheyenne on Number 4. Hang on to Grimes." He signed both his own name and Cortney's.

Miles Cortney wore a pale smile as Russ rejoined him. "You didn't show up any too soon, Russ. Look." He'd opened the paper to its classified ad section. One of the ads was about lost silver spurs.

17

Number 4, due in Cheyenne at 9:25 P.M., was on time. When Hyatt and Cortney stepped down from it a dozen men swarmed around them. They included Deputy Prosecutor Bliss, Sheriff Sharpless, the coroner, reporters from both the *Leader* and *Tribune*, and a WSGA lawyer named Sanford.

Bliss pounced on Russ. "What do you know about Grimes?"

"Where is he now?"

"In jail. But the evidence is hearsay and circumstantial. We can't hold him much longer. If you know anything, talk fast."

Anxiety on the face of the WSGA attorney, Sanford, made Russ hesitate. The association, he guessed, had scented a scandal and was worried about its effect on the market. Grimes was one of their members. That would explain Sanford's meeting the train. Instinctively Russ sympathized with him. It was hardly fair to punish a hundred honest cattlemen just because one, Wally Grimes, had padded his tally with intent to defraud. The newspaper men had poised pencils. If Russ made a full statement the whole world would know it by this time tomorrow.

"He had Mr. Cortney and me kidnapped." Russ

picked his words carefully. "I got away but Cort didn't. Skeets Carson caught up with them but they downed him. Then I had some luck and caught up with them myself."

They stood stunned and staring. The haggard, bruised face of Miles Cortney convinced them it was true. "A kidnapping? What for? Ransom?"

"Not ransom," Russ said. "If you send these newspaper fellas away I'll tell you all about it. Maybe you won't want it printed just yet. If you do, you can tell 'em yourself."

"Nix on that!" the *Tribune* man broke in. But Bliss overruled him. "Everybody stand aside," he ordered, "except the county officers." He got between Hyatt and Cortney, leading them to a deserted end of the platform. The sheriff and coroner followed.

"I think Mr. Sanford should know too," Russ suggested. "There's a reason. Now don't get sore, you fellas," he added as angry complaints came from the newsmen.

"All right," Bliss agreed impatiently. "You can come along, Sanford. Anything to start these witnesses talking."

The association lawyer joined them and in the dark shadow of the baggage room Russ told everything he knew about Wally Grimes. Cortney added a word here and there. "And right now," Russ finished, "Skeets is haulin' three dead men into Laramie."

Time and again the county officers broke in with questions. Worry grew on the face of Lawyer Sanford. "Look," he pleaded finally. "You've got a murder case against Grimes. That's all you need to hang him. No use bringing up the fraud case. It didn't go through. If you break it in the papers . . . ! Goshomighty! Can't you see what'll happen?"

The county officers didn't need to be told. It would panic investors all the way from Chicago to London. Herd after herd had changed hands by book count this past season. Many new stock issues were being floated. If the Grimes plot was exposed, many another big sale or promotion would fall under suspicion. Pending deals would freeze up. Herd speculation would stop dead. It was competition from speculators which had forced beef prices to six cents a pound. Without it, packing houses could buy at their own price and the livestock market might drop from six to three cents in a single day.

"And right before the fall shipping season!" Sanford argued desperately. "Don't you see? It could bust half the cowmen in Wyoming! And maybe both the Cheyenne banks!"

Prosecutor Bliss shook his head. "It's too big to cover up, Sanford. Six thousand head at thirty a round! Just by crossing two 'ones' in a tally book to make 'fours' out of them. That's the biggest rustling job on record. It makes every long-looper in Wyoming history look like a choir boy."

"But it didn't go through!" Sanford pleaded earnestly. "It fizzled, thanks to Hyatt here." He turned gratefully to Russ. "The Stockgrowers' Association won't forget it, either. You saved us from a gosh-awful mess."

Seth Sharpless said quietly: "The main thing I want now is to pick up the top rod in this deal. The man they call Lou. Maybe we can do that better if we stick to the murder charge and keep the long tally under our hats."

"But we can't make the murder charge stick," Bliss protested, "unless we show the motive. The motive is this big tally-book steal."

"All right," Sanford agreed, "bring it out at the trial. But the trial won't come up for a couple of months yet and by then the fall gather will be over and the fall beef will be shipped. New and honest counts will be in and made public. By then the WSGA will have expelled Grimes. We'll be shed of Grimes and his exposure at the trial won't contaminate the rest of us. . . ."

The argument went on, Russ missing part of it when a messenger handed him a note. As he read it through, a good deal of the tension left his face.

"We'll decide in the morning," Bliss was saying, "at the courthouse. I'll have my boss there; and either Judge Fisher or Judge Lee. Sanford, you can bring a committee from the WSGA. We want to be fair to them. And Mr.

Cortney, you and Hyatt be there at eight sharp."

"Make it nine, please," Russ begged. "Cort and I've got an eight-o'clock breakfast date."

From habit Russ wakened at six. He looked over at the other bed and saw that Cortney was still sleeping. A shame to wake him up! Registering at the Inter-Ocean they'd taken a double room for self-protection.

For murder would still hunt them, Russ knew, in or out of Cheyenne. They were witnesses. Key witnesses who could convict Grimes of murder. Grimes was in jail, but he had a partner who wasn't. A man known as Lou! Grimes wouldn't tell on Lou, because he'd want Lou free to work for him on the outside. Nor would Lou dare leave Grimes to his fate, for fear that Grimes in bitterness would expose him.

Only by killing off two key witnesses could Lou save Grimes. Skeets was less dangerous to them, because Skeets had run into only the French Creek bunch and had only hearsay knowledge of Grimes.

Who did Lou have to work with? At the last count he had Alford and Spoffard. Also a Boxed M tallyman named Shorty. Then Russ remembered that Lou himself could be a handy gunman. He could be Gerald Lorton. It was Lorton who'd challenged the winner after the famous rifle match between Major Talbot and

Skew Johnson. The major had won over Skew only to be outshot by Lorton.

Russ reached for his shirt and took a note from it. The one handed him at the depot last night.

> The suspense is killing us. Please tell us all about it at breakfast at my house at eight in the morning. Be sure to bring Mr. Cortney.
>
> GAIL GARRISON.

At first the "us" had puzzled Russ. But in the lobby they'd told him it was Gail Garrison and Jean Markle who'd found Clem Harwood's body. And that Jean was now Gail's guest at the Garrison house on upper Hill Street.

Russ jumped from bed and yanked covers from the other one. "Wake up, Cort, while I go down and find out when the barbershop opens. We need curryin', both of us, before we can show up in polite society."

The barbershop was open at seven. Newsmen pounced on them there, but from their questions Russ could tell they hadn't yet heard about a padded Boxed M tally. So Russ said nothing about it himself. From the first he'd been sure that Attorney Sanford's argument would win out. The WSGA was the mightiest power in Wyoming. It controlled the banks and the legislature. It would be sure to control this morning's policy meeting at the courthouse.

"We thought you'd gone hunting, Mr. Cortney," a *Leader* man said. "Just what happened to you, anyway?"

"I was held up and robbed," Cortney said. A doctor had treated his scalp wound last night.

"You want to know anything else," Russ put in, "go ask the sheriff."

An hour later he and Cortney rode up Hill Street in a hack. "Reckon I was the last man to see Clem Harwood alive," the hackman offered.

"Yeh?" Russ prodded. "How was that?"

"Hauled him home from the depot," the hackman said. "On the way he made me stop at the Carey Block. Went up the steps and somebody seen him go into Grimes' office. He was there quite a spell and then I drove him home. 'Bout a hour after that he was shot dead."

Gail and Jean met them at the door, excited and full of questions. "Begin at the beginning," Gail demanded.

Jean took Cortney's hat. She looked at bullet holes through it and then at his haggard face. "What did they do to you, Mr. Cortney?"

"Our names," Russ said, "are Cort and Russ. We don't answer to Mister. And first off, we got to know a few things ourselves. What were you gals doing over at Harwood's?"

Gail waited till they were at the table and

she'd poured coffee. "We went there first," she explained, "to show him this." She held up a copy of the decoy telegram. "So Uncle Clem went to Laramie to investigate. From there he wrote me this." She showed them the short note Harwood had sent by mail.

Two lines stood out and Russ read them aloud. " 'So it was rigged. By Wally Grimes, likely.' "

"When we found poor Uncle Clem dead," Gail said, "we went right to the sheriff. We showed him both the telegram and the letter."

"And told him about the buckboard," Jean added.

"And the boot laces," Gail put in.

"And the cigar stubs. And everything."

Bit by bit the girls gave their guests the chain of circumstantial evidence leading to Grimes' arrest. It showed that Harwood was checking on Grimes. He'd just left Grimes' office. He was shot with a .38 pistol; Grimes had owned an office gun of that calibre which couldn't be found now. Hyatt had been shot at by at least two men working for Grimes. Hyatt, tied up with Harwood's boot laces, had been hauled off in Grimes' buckboard. Finally, in checking a forged telegram at Laramie, Harwood had asked if Grimes or any of his crew had been seen lately around Laramie. Returning to Cheyenne he'd taken a hack directly to Grimes' office.

"But it wasn't enough," Gail said. "They were

about to turn him loose when your telegram came from Medicine Bow."

"And guess what cell he's in!" Jean Markle said.

"Not the one I had?" Russ exclaimed. "The one they dragged Mosier out of?"

"The very same," Jean said with a slight shiver.

The cook came in with breakfast and Gail waited till they were alone again. "Now tell us about *you*," she demanded. "We know part of it. It's all over town. But . . ."

"But you're holding something back, aren't you?" Jean prompted. "That's what the milkman told the cook this morning."

The men exchanged glances and Cortney nodded. "Okay, ladies," Russ said. "We're trustin' you. They want to keep the murder motive under a lid till the trial. There's a reason. But we'll let you in on it if you promise not to tell."

"We won't tell." Both girls gave the promise breathlessly.

"It'll all come out at the trial, couple of months from now," Russ said. Then he gave the complete story in quick, low words, stopping once for a slight correction from Cortney and again when the cook came in with more pancakes. "So the WSGA want us to keep the padded tally book out of it till trial day. They're afraid it might smash the market . . ."

"But that's not right!" Jean Markle broke in.

"News is news and truth is truth. The public shouldn't be cheated like that."

"But in the end they'll be told," Gail argued. "I can't see any harm in holding it back a month or two, Jean, if it will save hundreds of honest cattlemen from heavy losses; and the association from a disgrace it doesn't deserve."

The two girls, each sure she was right, continued to argue the ethics of it. As a crusading newswoman Jean Markle naturally took the side of giving every fact at once and frankly to the public. And Gail, a cattleman's daughter with close social ties to nearly every family in the WSGA, couldn't see it that way at all.

Miles Cortney stopped it by glancing at the clock and standing up. "In just five minutes," he reminded Russ, "we're due at the courthouse."

The girls went as far as the porch with them and there Russ turned to fix a searching gaze on Gail Garrison, "About this man Lou we heard them talk of. Any idea who he is?"

At once she was troubled and fearful. Something seemed to be on her mind which she couldn't bring herself to confide. She shook her head, her eyes not meeting Russ's. "It could be his first name or his last name," he persisted. "It could be spelled L o u i s or L e w i s. Know anyone with a handle like that, front or behind?"

"No," Gail said. She seemed on the point of

adding something. But Cortney was jogging Russ's arm. "We'll be late, Russ."

They went down the lawn walk to the gate. Russ opened it and they passed through. He waved to the girls on the porch and called out, "We'll let you know what they decide at the meeting."

He was relatching the gate when Cortney staggered and went down on one knee. Wood splintered at the gate post as from a block away, north up Hill Street, a rifle cracked twice. Russ's left arm caught Cortney to keep him from falling while his right hand brought a gun from his hip pocket. Coming here as a breakfast guest he'd left his belt and holster at the hotel.

Jean's cry from the porch echoed Gail's. Both girls came running to the gate. And Russ, looking up Hill Street, saw no one at all; nor heard anything. No third shot nor any hoofbeat of retreat. The street was empty.

18

Walking fretfully to the courthouse, half an hour later, Russ could reach only one conclusion. The boldness of this last try at his life seemed all but incredible. But desperation breeds boldness and he could imagine how desperate Gerald Lorton must be right now.

At a rifle match Lorton had once proved himself more expert than either of two famous marksmen. So from a block away he could confidently expect hits on two men, with two quick shots. Two men on the way to the courthouse to tell tales on Grimes! Grimes whose fate was wrapped up with Lorton's—if Lorton was Lou.

And who but Lorton would know about this eight-o'clock breakfast date at Gail's? Lorton who lived right around the corner on Twentieth, across from the public school. The shots had been fired from behind a high board fence beyond the schoolhouse playground. Nor had the sniper made off on a horse. He must have disappeared afoot to hide in some nearby house.

Who else could he be but Lorton?

Miles Cortney had been taken into Gail's house with a broken arm. Four inches to the right and the bullet would have found his heart. Hyatt's slight stoop to catch Cortney had saved his own life, the second bullet thudding into a gate post. A doctor was with Cortney now. Neighbors had helped Russ give chase to the sniper. They'd found only a pair of empty rifle shells back of the playground fence. Constable Nolan had joined them, promising to search nearby barns and houses. But what good would it do? Any man found in his own house certainly has a right to be there.

Russ took the courthouse steps two at a time and in the second-floor hall elbowed his way through men from the *Leader* and *Tribune*. They'd been barred from joining a group now assembled in the jury room. Russ was promptly admitted and found them waiting there—everyone but Seth Sharpless. The sheriff, upon hearing about the rifle shots on upper Hill Street, had gone to help Nolan beat about for the sniper.

Questions popped at Russ as he entered. "How's Cortney?" They all knew about the shooting but only Sharpless had left the meeting.

"Just a broken arm," Russ told them, looking around to see who was there. Besides the prosecutor and his staff there were two deputies, the coroner, Judge Fisher, Attorney Sanford and four members of the Wyoming Stockgrowers' Association.

What threw Russ off balance was seeing that one of the WSGA men present was Gerald Lorton. Although Lorton had sold the Boxed M a year ago he still kept up his association dues.

"How long've you been waitin' here?" Russ asked, his eyes on Lorton.

"We got here a few minutes before nine," Bliss said.

"*All* of you?" Confusion grew on Hyatt's face.

"All of us," Bliss said a little impatiently. "Now let's hear that story of yours again. About Grimes and his long tally."

Lorton's steel-green eyes met Russ's without wavering. He seemed tensely curious, just like the rest of them, on edge to hear the facts. And since he'd been here constantly since nine o'clock he couldn't have fired the shots.

Then Russ remembered something else. The rifle with which Lorton had outshot the winner of the Talbot-Johnson match, a year ago, was a Hotchkiss 45-70, 1879 model. The make and model had been publicized at the time by both local papers. The two empty shells just found back of a fence had been fired with a Winchester 44-40.

"Well?" Judge Fisher prompted sharply.

Russ came out of it and for the third time told the full story about Grimes. Pain and embarrassment scarred the faces of the association men as he described the doctored figures in a tally book.

Troubled talk broke out as Russ finished. "Sanford's right." "This could crack the market!"

"I know a dozen deals that'll blow up if this gets out." "Let's call a meeting and expel Grimes."

"That won't be enough, Jess. We've got to stave it off till the fall tallies are in and then certify 'em. We can't afford to break every cowman in Wyoming."

"I was afraid somethin' like this would happen," another fretted. "Any book-count deal's bad business, even when there's good faith. Tom Sturgis has been warnin' against it all along."

"We have a common interest, gentlemen," Attorney Sanford summed up. "It's to protect the dignity and integrity of the cattle industry in Wyoming. So let's keep this out of the papers until it breaks at the trial of Grimes—late in November."

The association invariably had its way in Wyoming. So Sanford's advice was adopted and all present were sworn not to give away facts about the padded tally book. "We'll stress the murder case," Bliss agreed, "and keep quiet about the fraud till court day."

A sudden memory made Russ break in. "Hold on. I turned a buckskin horse loose in Morton's Pass. A note hid in its mane tells all about the six thousand head overtally."

Again there was worry and confusion. One stockman wanted to start fifty cowboys looking for the buckskin, to recover and destroy the note.

"No good," another argued. "That's too many

cowboys to keep a secret. Better send just two men we can trust. How about you, Hyatt?"

"Sheets Carson and I could start out," Russ said, "just as soon as he gets here from Laramie. I look for him day after tomorrow."

A committee had already been rushed by train to Laramie, to help Skeets get a clearance and make sure he didn't talk about a padded tally. It was settled that Russ would start for the upper Sybille range as soon as Skeets was available to go with him. But Russ had something else on his mind. He waited till Sharpless got back and then drew the sheriff aside. "We didn't find that sniper," Sharpless reported.

"Grimes had three gunmen we can't account for," Russ said. "Spoffard, Alford and a roundup tallyman named Shorty. Might be any one of 'em."

"Not the tallyman," Sharpless thought. "The roundup camp's sixty miles north of here."

"But news of Grimes' arrest went there by stage. When he heard it Shorty might quit and head for Cheyenne."

"What for?"

"To get fresh orders from Lou."

"You're guessing, Hyatt."

"Sure I am. But somebody fired those rifle shots. And somebody else made it worth his while to do it."

The sheriff lighted a stogie, puffed it in a brown

study. "Looks like you'll be ducking slugs," he concluded, "till we get this whole gang locked up. You and Cortney both. I'll make out warrants for Spoffard, Alford and a Boxed M tallyman named Shorty. And while I'm at it, I can make out a John Doe warrant for 'Lou,' whoever he is."

"Look, sheriff," Russ argued. "Skeets and I are in this up to our necks. Why don't you deputize us and give us copies of those warrants? Then if we run into any of those four birds, we can make it official."

"You've got it coming," Sharpless admitted. "Couple of more fast-shooting deputies'll come in handy, right about now. So I'll sign you both on soon as Skeets hits town. Meantime . . ."

"Meantime," a voice broke in, "I've dug up a couple of more witnesses." Prosecutor Bliss appeared by them. "Pair of dude brothers named Apperson. Seems Grimes tried to saw off his long tally on *them,* too, soon as he lost Cortney."

"Where are they?" Sharpless asked.

"Packing to leave town on the first train. I made them promise not to give anything away. They were scared stiff when they heard about two other witnesses being shot at this morning."

The sheriff turned to Russ. "You know anything about these Appersons?"

"Never heard of 'em," Russ said.

"I don't think they'll be sniped at," Bliss brooded, "between now and train time. They know nothing about kidnapping or murder and they never heard the name Lou mentioned. It was Lou who took those shots this morning."

"Either him or somebody he gives orders to," Russ amended. "Have you asked Grimes who Lou is?"

"Fifty times. But he won't talk except to swear he didn't shoot Harwood."

An idea hit Russ and his eyes narrowed shrewdly. "Reckon I better go see how Cort's makin' out. If you need us, we got a room at Chase's hotel."

"Keep it bolted," Sharpless advised dryly, "till we pick up that rifleman."

Russ hurried to the hotel. Newspapermen hailed him in the lobby but he pushed past them. Going up to his room he found Cortney with his arm in a sling, reading today's *Leader*.

"How you doin', Cort?"

The Boston man grinned. "Don't give me a thought, Russ. The bone's set and all I have to do is keep quiet."

"And stay away from windows," Russ warned. "Lou's triggerman might take a shot from the street. What does the paper say about it?"

"Nothing about a tally book. It just says we were batted down in Harwood's cabin and hauled to the woods. Harwood got wind of it so they killed him."

"Anything about a motive?"

"It says the motive's known to the prosecutor but he wants to spring it as a surprise at the trial."

"Reporters been pesterin' you?"

Cortney grinned. "They knock on the door about once an hour."

"Next time they knock, let 'em in. And tell 'em about Judnick snitchin your money belt. How much did you say was in it?"

"Ten one-hundred dollar bills. But why tell about it?"

"You said they took eighty dollars pocket money off you. Then on the second night out Judnick found your money belt while Alford was rustlin' firewood. Chances are he didn't tell Alf anything about it. That thousand dollars was stashed on him, I bet, when they buried him at Morton's Pass."

On a cold dawn Russ and Skeets rode north out of Cheyenne. They were scabbard-armed and holster-armed, with four legal warrants in pocket and deputy-sheriff badges on their vests. A packed mule followed at the end of a lead rope. "By dark we can make the Y Bar," Russ said.

"Wonder if that buckskin's showed up there yet?"

"Maybe. But nobody's likely to find the note unless they curry his mane. My guess is he's still knee-deep in bluestem on upper Sybille."

"Find out anything more about that tallyman they call Shorty?"

Russ nodded. "He's on the Boxed M payroll as Shorty Goss. All the other Boxed M hands on the roundup are local boys, well known and okay. Yesterday a Campstool puncher rode in from the roundup and we asked him about Goss."

"What did he say?"

"He said Goss saddled up and rode south a few days back, and hasn't been seen since. It was right after they got news of Grimes' arrest."

Skeets thumped away his cigaret. "Anything else?"

"Yes. He said Shorty Goss rides with a Winchester 44-40; and he's a dead shot with it."

Russ and Skeets made the Schwartz station by noon and ate with passengers of two stages meeting there. Questions about Grimes volleyed at them. "Read about it in the *Leader*," Russ grinned, and tossed yesterday's copy to Schwartz.

"It says here," Schwartz announced to his guests, "that Judnick helped himself to that dude's money belt. Had a thousand dollars in it."

Russ and Skeets left the stage road a few miles beyond Pole Creek, angling northwest to hit Horse Creek at the Y Bar. Again the only man there was a choreman. "When you gonna fetch back that buckskin bronc?" the choreman asked as he set out a late supper in the cookshack.

"I'm on my way to pick it up right now," Russ said.

By sunup he and Skeets were asaddle and moving. Beyond the Y Bar they kept an alert watch for the buckskin. That afternoon they worked two high forks of the Chugwater on a line where timber met open grass. A few loose horses were grazing there but the buckskin wasn't among them.

"We can't fuss around too long," Russ said, "else Spoff and Alf'll beat us to the Pass."

"Where d'yuh reckon they are?" Skeets asked as they made camp for the night.

"Not at the Boxed M because the sheriff looked for them there. Might be they hid out in the hills. Or maybe they high-tailed for Montana. Only thing I'm sure of is they're readin' everything printed about Grimes. You can buy a Cheyenne *Leader* most anywhere."

Skeets chuckled. "I'd like to see their faces when they find out they buried Judnick with all that dough on him."

"They could easy do it," Russ argued. "It was dim dawn and they were in a sweat to move on. Not likely they thought to rip open the lining of his jacket."

After a starlight sleep they crossed a rise to slopes where forks of the Sybille spread out like the fingers of a hand. Russ rode up one fork and down another, while Skeets went up a third and down a fourth. At sundown they met with no news of the buckskin. "Might have drifted toward

Pole Mountain," Russ said, "which is farther than we got time to look right now."

Morton's Pass was only a few miles on and they worked that way early in the morning. "There's the hill where they had me treed, Skeets."

On the west side of it they came to a small gully. "Judnick cashed in right here," Russ said.

Skeets looked at the lay of land. "Quickest way to get him outa sight," he concluded, " 'd be to tote him to that patch of woods." He thumbed toward aspens a little north of the butte.

"Being in a hurry," Russ reasoned, "they wouldn't tote him an inch further'n they had to." With Skeets he rode on the shortest line to the woods and dismounted.

Moving afoot into the trees they circled about, kicking in dry leaves. Sunlight filtered through the autumn-gold foliage overhead.

"Here she is," Skeets announced.

He stood by what was plainly a grave, hurriedly dug and covered. Near it were a few cigaret butts and bootprints.

"It's Judnick, all right," Skeets said. "Shall we dig him up?"

Russ shook his head. "We'll leave that to Spoff and Alf."

They made camp a half a mile away and took turns watching from a high lookout. Three days dragged by and no one came.

"We figgered 'em wrong," Skeets concluded on the fourth day.

"Maybe they got a coupla hundred miles away," Russ argued, "before they ran into a Cheyenne paper. For a thousand dollars they'd ride back twice that far. Take 'em the best part of a week."

"Or maybe Jud divvied with Alf after all."

"That would make him honest," Russ said.

A morning later he went to the lookout to relieve Skeets.

"Never mind," Skeets said, pointing west. Two riders were coming uphill from the Laramie Plains. One rode a blazed-face sorrel.

"Spoff had a bronc like that, last I saw of him," Russ remembered. "Let's go meet 'em, Skeets."

19

They were at the aspen grove well ahead of the oncomers. Russ found a dead windfall and got back of it, flat to the ground. Skeets crouched a little to the left. Hoof sounds told them that horsemen were approaching at a walk.

"Let 'em get through digging first," Russ said.

The horsemen dismounted just outside the trees. "Look at the time we wasted." The sandpaper voice was Alford's. "All because you were in such a sweat to get outa here."

"Quitcher crybabyin' and fetch along that shovel."

They came into the trees, Alford with a short-handled spade. The blackness of his shirt matched his hat and holster and boots—and the black, shiny stubble on his face and chin. The man with him was chunky, wearing a gray hat and brown jacket. Both had bloodshot eyes and the look of men who'd made a fast, forced ride through wind and sun.

"It was right about here," Spoffard said uncertainly. "No," Alford thought, "over this way a little."

Russ raised to hands and knees to see over the windfall. Both men stopped suddenly, alert, Spoffard's hand on his gun. Once, Russ remembered, he'd been a man-killing Kansas marshal.

"You hear anything, Spoff?" Dry leaves had crackled under Hyatt's knees.

"A squirrel, likely. Start diggin'."

Alford scraped leaves from the grave and began digging. It didn't take long. The grave was shallow and its occupant was soon exposed. "Rip the jacket, Alf."

Alford dropped to his knees. When he stood up again there was money in his hand. "Just like the paper said, Spoff. An even thousand." He passed half of it to Spoffard.

"All right. Cover him up and we'll fan outa here."

Russ waited till they'd refilled the grave. When they turned their backs to walk out to their horses he signalled Skeets. Both cowboys stood up with level guns.

"The funeral's over," Russ announced. "And better not start another one. It might turn out to be yours."

Spoffard froze, his hands not up but reaching forward, palms away from him. Alford whirled and made a half-draw. It ended in a yelp as a bullet from Skeets raked his shoulder. "Better take it easy," Russ warned them. "We've got warrants and badges to back 'em up."

The shoulder pain dropped Alford to his knees; from there he went forward to one hand, the other clutching at his wound. Spoffard hadn't moved. His back was still this way, his palms spread forward. He was like a stiff, silent statue. All the groans and cursing came from Alford.

Russ stepped over the windfall and advanced toward them. "It was you started all this, Blackie. Remember? You and that dry-gulching saddle gun of yours. Wrap him up, Skeets."

It looked easy as Skeets picked up Alford's gun and Russ punched his own into the middle of Spoffard's back. "You're lettin' us down," Skeets complained. "We thought you'd put up a fight."

"Only time they can fight," Russ said, "is when the other fella's not lookin'."

He was reaching to take Spoffard's forty-five from its holster when the man's spurred heel kicked back hard. It was a long-roweled Spanish spur and caught Russ on the shin. A knife-stab there wouldn't have hurt worse and in the instant of torture Russ Hyatt's legs doubled under him.

In the same split second Spoffard drew and jumped behind a tree, shooting. A bullet licked Hyatt's cheek and the pain at his shin did the rest. He went off balance and down, landing flat on his chest, still holding his gun but in no position to shoot.

The shooting was above and over him. Guns roared at his right and left and Skeets yelled, "Stay down, Russ."

Another tongue of flame licked out across

Russ. He kept still for a moment, then crawled from the line of fire. He looked up to see Skeets blowing through the bore of his forty-five. Alford grovelled, still nursing and cursing a bloody shoulder. Spoffard lay jack-knifed back of his tree. His gun hand was empty and gray death was creeping up his face.

A noon later, after a pushing ride, they sighted Horse Creek with the Y Bar meadows spread out along it. Alford clung to the horn of his saddle, his face tight with pain, the torn shoulder in desperate need of attention. "One of us better stay at the Y Bar with him," Russ decided, "while the other rides for a doctor."

Spoffard was long past suffering. His canvas-covered body was lashed to the saddle of his blazed-face sorrel.

As they trailed nearer to the Y Bar Russ reined to an alert stop. "You see what I see, Skeets? In the corral?"

"I see a buckskin horse," Skeets said.

"The same one, on a bet!" Russ spurred on to the ranch.

An excited choreman met them at the corral. "You been holdin' out on me, Hyatt! Howcome you rid by here twice without lettin' me in on it?"

"Letting you in on what?"

"About Wally Grimes! Him and his long tally. A six-thousand head overcount, done deliberate.

Criminy! It'll blow the roof plumb off the Cheyenne Club!"

Russ looked at the buckskin, saw that it had been stabled and curried. "Who brought it in?" Skeets asked.

"Coupla Y Bar boys ran into it on Sybille. They needed a fresh mount so they tossed a rope. And found that note of yourn, Hyatt. Who you got there on that . . . ?"

"Where is it now?" Russ cut in.

"They high-tailed to Cheyenne with it," the choreman said, his eyes bugging at the two led horses. "Caught up with 'em, didja? They're Boxed Ms, ain't they?"

Russ nodded and slid from his horse. "One dead and one kicking. If that buckskin's fresh, I'll borrow him again and light out for Cheyenne."

The tortured Alford was taken to a bunk and Spoffard, tarp-covered, was laid in the saddle room. While the buckskin was being grained for a long fast ride, the choreman fed Russ at the cookshack. "You're right," Russ brooded. "It'll blow the roof off. And I want to be there when it happens. Skeets, you stay here and work on Blackie. Keep askin' him who Lou is."

So far it had done no good. Skeets called to the bunk with the same question. Alford cursed him and shrieked back: "Never heard of him. Quitcher naggin' and get me a doctor."

"I'll send a doctor from Cheyenne," Russ promised.

"He's sure a slick one!" the choreman marveled. "I mean that guy Grimes. I've heard of stealin' one steer. Or a hundred. But when he padded that tally he figgered to steal six thousand! Goshomighty! Once I saw a guy strung up fer stealin' only *one!*"

By early afternoon Russ was on the buckskin, spurring for Cheyenne. It wasn't hard to imagine the impact of the news there. The shock and the scandal of it. The consternation in bank circles. Checkbooks freezing up as many a pending deal stopped dead between two strokes of a pen! The stark truth about a padded tally. If one tally was padded, suspicion was sure to fall on others. How far would the beef market drop at Omaha and Chicago?

Pressure on Grimes would redouble to make him identify Lou. Gerald Lorton? Russ, racing on, had no doubt of it. But proving it was something else. And what about Lorton himself? Would he brazen it out? Or had he already made tracks from Cheyenne?

The last thought gave wings to Hyatt, sent him pounding on and brought him to the Pole Creek station just after sundown. At this hour no stage was stopping there, so only Schwartz and his wife and a wrangler took supper with Russ. At first sight of him they began firing questions. They knew about the note in the buckskin's mane. The two Y Bar riders had stopped here on their way to deliver it at Cheyenne.

"Addressed to the sheriff, wasn't it?" Schwartz prodded. "And to Tom Sturgis and the Stockgrowers' bank?"

There was no use denying it. Clearly the messengers were telling the world about it. It would be bruited about at every bar in town.

"It'll sure stand 'em on their haids!" the wrangler predicted. "Folks wouldn't believe them Gonzales brothers, when they hit town the other day. Thought it was just spite talk from a coupla sorehaids. It'll be different now. After this they'll believe *anything* on Grimes."

Russ looked up from his supper, puzzled. "Gonzales brothers?"

"They're from Old Mex," the wrangler explained. "Seems news about Grimes' arrest on a murder charge made papers all over the country. Couple of fire-eaters from Mexico showed up in Cheyenne and paid a call on Grimes at the jail. They stood right in front of that cage and spit through the bars at him. 'A *ladron*!' they called him. Then they spilled some dirt to the sheriff."

"On Grimes?"

"Yeh, they claimed he married their sister and then made off with her cows. They said they been lookin' fer him ever since."

It wasn't quite dark when Russ rode on. He followed the stage road across open prairie. Light faded and stars came out. Exactly four weeks ago he'd taken this same road, at this same hour, on a blue roan. A roan he'd bought to replace the mount shot out from under him by Alford. That was the day he'd met Gail Garrison on the stage—the day she saw his rough-and-tumble in the stage yard. How often she'd been in his thoughts since then!

Nine miles of jogging and he saw the shapes of two windmills and a dark house. The Seeley stage-house and again its people were asleep. Right here he'd caught up with Skeets Carson.

An odd sense that history was repeating came to Russ. Like he'd traveled in a circle, these last four weeks, and was now back at the same beginning.

An hour later the feeling came to him again when he saw the lights of Fort Russell off to his right. The lights winked out. He heard a distant bugle blowing taps.

Skeets had left him here, angling toward the TOT.

Again, as then, Russ kept straight on and was soon riding down a dark street in the north suburbs of Cheyenne. He passed the fairgrounds and rode on by some of the big, fine town houses built along here by Wyoming cattle kings. Per capita the richest city in the world, they said of

Cheyenne. And the wickedest! according to Jean Markle.

Russ struck Eddy Street at Twenty-first and turned south there. Then a rumble of sound came to him. Again a sense of repeated history troubled him—for the sound had a sinister tone! It whipped his mind back to four weeks ago tonight, on September 11th, as he'd ridden down this same street at this same hour.

At Twentieth he saw them. A mob of men a block south at the corner of Nineteenth and Eddy. More than a hundred of them and Russ knew at once what was up. A man's terrified scream reached him. And a jumble of voices.

"That-there telegraph pole'll do."

"Toss yer rope over it."

"It's the one we used fer Mosier, ain't it?"

"Why not? We took him from the same cage, didn't we?"

"Quitcher whinin', Grimes, and start sayin' yer prayers."

Russ reined up short, his heart thumping, tugs pulling at him two ways. If ever a man needed hanging it was Wally Grimes. Nor was it hard to understand why these bar bums would do it. Scarcely a one of them but had known a man of their own kind who'd swung for stealing *just one cow.* Now here was a big brand owner who'd stolen *two great herds.* One from a deserted wife in Mexico. The other a paper herd which had never existed at all; a try at rustling the value of six thousand steers merely by faking a tally.

"If it was me done it," a man yelled, "I'd've been h'isted long ago." Class jealousy was breaking out on these men, like pocks on the skin. "Yeh," another jeered, "just because he belongs to the champagne crowd ain't no reason he ortn't be treated same as anybody else. Let's git done with it and go to bed."

Then the opposite tug pulled at Russ. There was a badge on his vest. One he'd asked for himself. To get it, he'd had to give an oath to uphold the law.

This wasn't law—this ugly, bestial thing in front of him. It was high treason against every decent conception of law. No man ever needed hanging more than Grimes; yet no town ever needed the law, in its cleanest sense, more than Cheyenne.

Anger boiled in Russ and he spurred to the edge of the crowd. "Where's the sheriff?" he asked a man there.

The man snickered. In the dark he couldn't see Russ's badge. "Him and his crew tuk off on a bum tip we gave him—that Shorty Goss is hidin' in a hay shed up Crow Crik. Time he gets back . . ."

"Where's the mayor?" Russ broke in impatiently. He remembered four weeks ago tonight when Mayor Joe Carey had appeared here, half dressed, to plead in vain against the lynching of Mosier.

"He's out to his CY ranch to see'f it's still there." Again the man snickered. "Folks ain't sure of nothin' after what Grimes almost got away with."

A shriek from Grimes split the night, choked off as they lifted him clear of the ground. Beyond him Russ saw two unfamiliar faces, round and shining and foreign. The dark, gloating faces of men too strangely alike to be anything but brothers.

Russ remembered a name spoken at the Schwartz station. Gonzales!

"*Arriba!*" one of them shouted; it was like a cheer at a bull fight. Russ knew the idiom and it meant "Up with him!"

"*Mas arriba!*" the other brother yelled; meaning "Higher!"

But the men at the rope let Grimes to the ground again, giving him the same cruel play they'd given Mosier.

"*Arriba!*" demanded the first Gonzales. His black eyes snapped vindictively, yet clearly he was enjoying himself; as though this revenge was even sweeter than the one he'd hoped for. "*Arriba!*" he cried again.

And again up went Grimes into the air, kicking, his face purplish and bloated.

Russ pulled his forty-five and spurred through

the crowd, the force of his charge brushing men right and left. Absorbed with the kicking Grimes they barely saw Hyatt till he was at the rope, his horse rearing there. Russ pressed the muzzle of his gun against the taut rope, a foot above Grimes' head, and squeezed the trigger.

The rope snapped and Grimes fell in a heap.

Russ stood in his stirrups, whirled his horse as the mob pressed around him. A hum of surprise grew to resentment and then swelled to a roar of fury. "Who is he?" "Yank him off that bronc!" "Toss a loop over him, somebody, and drag him out of the way."

Russ fired twice into the air and the shots quieted them for a moment. He couldn't hold them off long and he knew it. Couldn't, that is, unless he gave them a solid compelling reason for sparing Grimes.

"Listen, men," Russ shouted. "Grimes is only second fiddle. The top fiddle is somebody named Lou. But who's Lou? Nobody knows but Grimes. You hang Grimes and Lou goes scot-free."

For a breath or two Russ waited, hoping for a ripple of support. All he got was sullen silence. A silence broken suddenly by two Latin voices shouting lustily, "*Arriba*! *Arriba*."

"I'm a deputy sheriff," Russ said, "with a warrant for Lou. I want to serve it tonight. But I'll never know who Lou is unless you let Grimes tell me. You wouldn't cheat me out of that, would you? You don't want to let this guy Lou get away, do you? Bad as Grimes is, Lou's a heap worse."

The silence smouldered. Then somebody said, "It's that cowboy Hyatt." Another said, "It was him turned up Grimes." Another said: "Anyway we had our fun. He sure put on a dance, Grimes did."

The crisis snapped. The crowd began melting away as Russ sat there on the buckskin horse, his heart pounding under the badge on his vest. Grimes cringed at his stirrup. "Take me back!" he begged in a sob-choked voice. "Take me back to jail!"

Even the filthiest cage on earth, that night, was heaven to Wally Grimes.

20

When Russ pushed him into it, minutes later, it was still the same five-by-seven kennel that had held Mosier. Inmates of the other boxes stared fearfully and then a jailer appeared, his face the shade of skimmed milk.

"They took my keys," he whimpered. "I couldn't help it. Honest..."

"Never mind. Go dig up a policeman or somebody. Right now I want five minutes alone with Grimes."

The five minutes brought nothing from Grimes. "Never heard of him!" was all Russ could get out of the man. Already a sort of low cunning was replacing his panic. He seemed to reason that once the law knew Lou's identity, the law would have no further motive to save him from mob violence. They who'd snatched him from this cage might come to do it again.

"Maybe the Gonzales boys know," Russ said in the end. "I'll look 'em up."

The jailer came back with one of Nolan's men. Russ advised them to bolt all doors and stand guard. Then he went out to his horse and rode down Ferguson. It was eleven at night with the town wide awake and seething. Men huddled on street corners, in dim doorways, whispering, waiting. The drama of a lynching had put them on edge. The word ran riot, down Eddy and up Ferguson and back down Hill, that Russ Hyatt had saved Grimes and was now hunting bigger game—a mystery man named Lou.

The sidewalks stared as Russ rode by. His own eyes searched right and left for two swarthy brothers named Gonzales. Since they knew about Grimes, they might also know about Lou.

They'd seemed well dressed and prosperous. Probably they'd arrived by train and had put up at the best hotel. So at Sixteenth Russ turned a block east to the Inter-Ocean, tying at the hitchrail there.

He went into the lobby, gaunt, trail-weary, his gun-holster open and flat on his thigh. A buzz of talk stopped as he entered. It was plain that everyone here knew the story of the night. Quick voices had carried it to every corner of Cheyenne.

Two in the lobby moved toward him. At the time it didn't seem strange at all that they came hand in hand. Emotion ran high that night in Cheyenne and perhaps they didn't know it themselves. One was a man from Boston with an arm in a sling. The other was a girl from New York, darkly lovely, a vivid, brown-eyed girl stirred just now by deep feeling.

"We heard," she said breathlessly. "And we're proud. It was grand of you, Russell Hyatt." In the sparkling eyes of Jean Markle he'd done much, tonight, to heal the shame of Cheyenne. She dropped Cortney's hand and took both of Hyatt's.

The Boston man wore a self-conscious grin. "My sentiments exactly, Russ."

A dozen questions surged up in Russ but only one came to his lips. "You know whether a coupla Mexicans are registered here? Name's Gonzales."

"Yes," Jean said at once. "Twins, I imagine, with the most polite manners I ever saw. Are they important?"

Something seemed to be on Cortney's mind. "When you get time, Russ, I want to . . ."

"There they are now," Jean broke in, looking toward the Hill Street entrance. Two swarthy little men, wearing broad velvet hats and braided jackets, were just coming in.

" 'Scuse me," Russ said, and headed toward them.

He met them at the foot of the stairs and asked bluntly, "You fellas know Wally Grimes?"

They saw the badge on his vest, then looked up at him with a stiff respect. Clearly they recognized him as an officer who'd just cut down Grimes. One of them said cautiously: "It gives us no pride, señor. He is a man of evil who brought a great wrong to our house."

"I'll take your word for it," Russ said. "What about a fella named Lorton? Gerald Lorton?"

The brothers exchanged glances. "Do we know such a man, Ernesto?"

"Lorton?" Ernesto brooded. "The name seems familiar, Manuel . . . I have it! He stands up with Grimes on the day of our shame. He is *caballero mejor* . . . what is it you say, best man? . . . at the marriage of our sister."

"True, Ernesto. When I think of it I am sad. I remember our dear sister speaks of him as *'Don Luis.'*"

"She called him *Don Luis?*" Excitement flushed Russ and a sense of climax struck him. "That's all I want to know. Thanks."

He left them and hurried out to his horse. He'd stepped into the saddle before he noticed that Cortney and Jean Markle had followed to the sidewalk. "When you get time, Russ," Cortney began again, "I'd like to . . ."

"Right now time's aburnin', Cort." Russ waved to them and loped away, north up Hill.

Don Luis! It was exactly the title a Mexican lady would give to a well-dressed American whose intimates called him "Lou." Beyond any shadow of doubt Lorton was Lou.

Where would he be right now? Riding hard for parts unknown? Or maybe hiding like a cornered fox in his house? Tonight's lynching party was sure to panic him. For Grimes, to save his rope-burned neck, might at any minute name him as Lou. And Lorton by now must know that the Gonzales brothers were in town.

His house was on Twentieth between Hill and Ransome. Right around the corner from the Garrison place. Was Gail up yet? It still lacked half an hour of midnight.

And this was a night when few slept in Cheyenne. Windows showed light and men still whispered on the walks. Phrases of talk reached Russ.

"Grassers dropped a penny a pound at Chicago."

"Bet they skid another cent tomorrow."

"Look! There he goes now."

"Who?"

"The man on the buckskin horse. Russ Hyatt."

Hyatt's was a name to conjure with, tonight in Cheyenne. The man who'd dragged into daylight the scandal of a padded tally! The man on a buckskin horse who'd stopped the lynching of Grimes.

A group at the Opera House corner saw him ride by. "Hey there, Hyatt!" a whisky-flushed stockman called out. "Who's this Lou they're talkin' about?"

Russ had no time for talk. He spurred on up Hill.

Beyond Eighteenth the walks were empty. At Nineteenth the Congregational Church loomed in the dark. Beyond it the spiked iron fence of the Garrison lawn reached all the way to Twentieth. One of its lower windows had a light and leading to it Russ saw a bricked path lined with lilacs. Only a week ago he'd taken breakfast here with Gail and Jean and Cort.

"Russ!" He heard his name called softly and saw a figure in white, with a dark shawl around her shoulders, emerge from the lilac path and stand by the gate.

He stepped from the saddle and dropped the reins. When he crossed the sidewalk she reached both hands across the gate to him. "Gail! Have you heard about . . . ?"

"Everyone has," she broke in. "I'm glad you didn't let them do it." She looked at his badge and then raised her eyes, moist and shining, to meet his own. "But you've done enough, Russ." Her voice had an anxious plea in it. "Please let others do the rest."

He had to tell her something and wanted to get it over with quickly. "The rest is to find Lorton." It sounded blunt and flat. He'd dreaded telling her about Lorton.

But strangely she didn't seem shocked or even startled. It was as though she'd known all along about Lorton. The anxious, earnest plea was still in her voice and eyes. "Let the sheriff find him," she begged. "Or Nolan and his constables. Please!"

He stared across the gate at her. "You mean you *knew?* That Lorton's in it with Grimes?"

"I didn't really know," Gail said quickly. "I had

a vague suspicion. But I didn't really know till an hour ago."

"An hour ago? What happened?"

"I was standing at this gate when he passed on his way home. He was on foot and running and he looked deathly afraid. It was just after they'd dragged Grimes from his cell. I called to Gerry but he didn't stop. He ran on and turned the corner toward his house."

Russ dropped her hands and crossed the walk to his horse. "I got to pick him up. He'll be gone if I don't."

She came through the gate and stood at his stirrup as he mounted. "Please don't. He'll fight. I know him. He'll fight you with a gun. And haven't you done enough? Enough riding and fighting . . . You're tired. You ought to be in bed, Russ Hyatt. . . . Oh, why must you be so stubborn?"

"What's started needs finishing," Russ said. "He won't be any trouble, Gail. It's late. You better go inside."

He loped on up the block to Twentieth and turned east out of her sight there.

The third house from the corner was the picket-fenced cottage where Lorton kept bachelor quarters. It looked dark and deserted, the window shades drawn. Was Lorton hiding inside?

Russ tied the buckskin in front. He passed through the picket gate and crossed a small garden to the porch. The door had a knocker and he rapped sharply with it. No one answered. Yet Lorton had come running here only an hour ago, driven in terror by what had happened to Grimes.

Russ tried the door and it was bolted. Should he crash in? He had a John Doe warrant for "Lou." And Lou was Lorton.

The front porch had a window. It was locked. Russ circled to the back yard. The rear door was bolted but when he tried a nearby window it gave. He pushed the sash up. The catch at the top hadn't been latched.

Russ reached in and raised the blind. Beyond was blackness. He heard nothing. Yet he felt sure that Lorton was somewhere in the house. "I'm coming in after you, Lou!" Russ called out. He expected no answer and none came. But it assured him that Lorton wasn't in this back room. If there, he would have fired as Russ stood framed against starlight at the window.

Getting a leg over the sill, Russ climbed awkwardly in. He struck a match and saw he was in a kitchen. A soiled plate and cup meant that one man had eaten supper here. The match showed him a candle. He lighted the candle and in this brighter glow saw a burning cigaret. A half-smoked cigaret still fired at one end!

So Lorton was still here! Less than three minutes ago he'd been in this kitchen. With a candle in one hand and a drawn gun in the other, Russ began a circuit of the house.

Any door he opened could draw a shot. Behind one of them Lorton was cringing—but not too frightened to let loose bullets at Hyatt.

There were four rooms and Russ explored them one by one. A stray letter on the parlor table caught Russ's eye. He paused a moment to read it by candlelight. It was addressed to Gerald Lorton on stationery of Schoverling, Daly and Gates, arms dealers of 84 Chambers Street, New York.

> As per your order we're shipping you one 45-70 Hotchkiss repeater carbine, model 1883. This is a bolt action piece weighing 85 ¾ pounds, and with a barrel length of 22 ½ inches. We're confident you'll find it even more accurate than the 1879 model we sent you two years ago.

It was enough to remind Russ that the man he hunted was the best rifle shot in Wyoming.

He circled back to the kitchen. Did the place have a cellar? He opened a door and saw steep, descending steps.

"Lou!" he called down them. His call drew no shot nor any other answer from Lou.

"I'm coming down there after you, Lou." But Russ knew it would be suicide to walk down those steps with a lighted candle in hand. Lorton would shoot him from the dark.

So he blew out the candle. When it stopped smoking he put it in a side pocket of his coat. Then he took off his boots.

In inky darkness he began groping down the steps, slowly, planting each next step deliberately so he wouldn't make a board creak. His bootless feet had no spurs to clink. Russ moved silently on down, gun out and the butt braced against his ribs. He couldn't doubt that Lorton was down there. Once on the level cellar floor he'd at least be on equal terms with the man.

He was almost at the bottom when his foot kicked something. A fruit jar fell from the step and crashed on the floor. The shock of sound made a man down there begin shooting. A flash of flame stabbed at Russ and he fired back at it, bending double to lessen his height.

The other gun flashed again, and again Russ fired back. He took the last two steps at a blind jump and crouched low on the cellar floor. From there he fired twice and heard the man fall. No other sound came from him.

Russ shifted sidewise in the darkness, then advanced cautiously, groping. His fingers touched a wall. He slid along it, holding his breath. Lorton could still be alive with a cocked gun.

Another step forward and Hyatt's groping

hand touched flesh. The flesh didn't move. He couldn't doubt that it was Lorton and that Lorton was dead.

Russ took the candle from his pocket, lighted it, gave a long look. Then quietly he left the cellar. In the kitchen he put on his boots. He let himself out at the front and went to his horse. The public school loomed darkly across the street. Russ reloaded his gun and swung to the buckskin's saddle. He rode west to Ferguson and there turned a block south to the courthouse.

Chief Constable Nolan stood in front of it.

"There's a dead man in Gerald Lorton's cellar," Russ told him.

Nolan's eyes bugged. "Who? Lorton?"

"No. Shorty Goss. Take care of him, will you? While I go find Lorton."

"What do you want *him* for?"

"Got a warrant for him. His other name's Lou." Russ didn't even dismount. He loped on to Seventeenth and turned east.

Three blocks that way took him to the Cheyenne Club and he tied at a rack there.

21

It was midnight but the place was lighted upstairs and down. All the club hitchrails were lined with rigs and saddle mounts. A tallyho was drawn up at one, its six horses stamping restlessly. Oelrichs' outfit, and Russ wasn't surprised to see it here. On this night of crisis every member within miles would be in to learn the latest about Grimes.

Russ went up the main steps, spurs clinking on the boards. Again he found the entrance invitingly open. Members and messengers had been passing in and out all evening, and Russ, going in, met a telegraph boy coming out. And again he wasn't surprised. Stockholders all over the world would be wiring here, asking about book counts. Was the Boxed M the *only* one padded, they'd want to know—and get little sleep till they learned the truth.

Russ crossed an entrance hall to the main lounge. For a moment he stood unnoticed in its draperied arch. A hearth fire blazed with more than a dozen brand owners sitting around it. A few were wind-burned veterans. Others were young adventurers with the stamp of Oxford or Harvard. Russ recognized two titled Englishmen who'd invested fortunes in Wyoming cattle.

Some were rich in fact; others were rich only on paper. Some owed notes at the banks and a three-cent drop in the beef market would wipe them out.

Every man of them looked grim, this night when the bubble of a false prosperity burst in Cheyenne.

Maybe they'd blame it on him, Russ thought, and braced himself for a cool reception.

Then young Hugh Calvert turned and saw him there. Calvert had come out from Maryland two years ago to invest an inherited fortune in cattle. He kept a permanent room at the club and they'd put him on the house committee; sometimes he acted as host in the absence of President Phil Dater. Russ knew him only by sight; had heard of him as a popular young aristocrat who could lead a Lancers' reel more handily than he could rope a cow.

Calvert's quick and genuine welcome surprised him. He crossed to Russ and took his hand warmly. "You're Hyatt, I believe? We were just talking about you. Congratulations on turning up Grimes." He called to a steward. "Thomas, fetch in some Champagne Rocdeau. This is an occasion."

Others crowded around Russ, none of them less cordial than Calvert. With some it was a glum, half-sheepish cordiality but it was none the less genuine. Instead of resentment Russ heard apology. "We should have spotted Grimes ourselves, Hyatt," one said. Another drooped his lips in a wry smile. "Serves us right, maybe. Some of us've done a little book-tally tradin' ourselves. We didn't mean any harm. But maybe it gave Grimes his idea."

They're game! Russ thought. Dead game losers compelling his respect and admiration. Men like this would bounce back and build a greater Wyoming. Then he realized that as yet they knew nothing about Gerald Lorton. Lorton, too, was a member here.

Before he could tell them, Thomas came in with champagne. It was bubbling Rocdeau except for one stiff brandy handed to H. W. (Hard Winter) Dorn of Rawhide Buttes, whose contempt for French wines was well known.

When all were served, Hugh Calvert offered a toast. "To our guilty consciences, gentlemen, for condoning the code of trading by the book. May it teach us a lesson, so that never again will this scandal be repeated in Wyoming!"

They all drank and only one man seemed to choke on it. He was a Powder River man in deep at the banks, likely to be bankrupted by today's market dive.

"Cheer up," one of the older men said. "It would be a lot worse if Grimes had put his deal over. He didn't. Hyatt nipped it in the bud. My money says the market'll drop two cents, but not three. She'll be on her way up again by the time we ship in November."

"You only know part of it," Russ told them. "Grimes has a silent partner who put him up to it. His name's Gerald Lorton and I've a warrant for his arrest. The charge is murder, kidnapping and fraud."

They were still game and took it standing up.

Hard Winter Dorn gave a snort. "So we got *two* black sheep, 'stead of only one! You figure he's hiding here, do you? Well, he isn't."

Hugh Calvert spoke quietly. "You have our permission, Hyatt, to search the club, roof to cellar."

"That's what I came here for," Russ admitted. "But I don't need to now. You say he's not here, and your word's as good as gold. Thanks, fellas. I'll go look for him someplace else."

He left them and hurried out. Again his spurs clinked on the steps and then he was asaddle, riding the buckskin back down Seventeenth.

Where should he next look for Lorton? Gail had seen him less than two hours ago, which was after the passing of the last train through Cheyenne. Unless the man had left on horseback he was still in town.

The livery barns were on the west side, so Russ cantered that way. At each stable he could ask if Lorton had called for a horse.

He was heading for the IXL when lights from

a saloon made him pull up short. Voices from inside meant that the place was full of customers. It was sure to be on a night like this, for Colonel Luke Murrin's bar was the most popular in town.

Always it had been a hub of information. And usually the information was reliable. Rumors focused here and when a thing happened in Cheyenne, Luke Murrin generally learned about it before anyone else. His liquor was priced higher, and was served in finer glassware than his competitors used. But with it went a running comment on up-to-the-minute news and gossip, delivered free by the Colonel himself. Men said of Murrin that he saw all, heard all, knew all. Tonight he might even know the whereabouts of Gerald Lorton.

So Russ dismounted and went in. His entrance wasn't noticed because customers were facing the rear where Luke Murrin stood toying with the gold chain that spanned his immaculate white vest, rocking back and forth on his heels as he dispensed tidbits from his store of wisdom. Men at bar and tables hung on his words.

"That's right, gentlemen. This Boston man Cortney says he'll buy the Boxed M after all." Murrin waxed expansively mellow as he hooked thumbs in his armpits and gave out the news. "That is, he'll bid it in on the basis of a true cattle count at the current market price. The bank holds paper against it and will insist on a sale. And after what he's been through, no one will bid against Cortney. Which means he'll pick up a bargain."

"How good a bargain, Luke?" a customer asked.

Russ pulled his hatbrim over his eyes and stood quietly at the front, eyes down as he rolled a cigaret. No one had recognized him and he hoped they wouldn't. Now he remembered meeting Cortney and Jean Markle earlier tonight in the hotel lobby. Twice Cort had tried to tell him something; but he'd broken away to pump the Gonzales brothers about Lou. *So he'll take over the Boxed M, after all! That's what he wanted to tell me.*

"Figure it out yourselves," Murrin went on, his round pink face wise and smiling. "He'll get the outfit on a *true* count at about twenty a head, instead of on a padded count at thirty a head. He saves close to a quarter million dollars and gets exactly the same herd of cattle. And who can he thank for it? None other than Russ Hyatt!"

Russ flushed to the ears, pulling his hatbrim still lower.

"He's plenty grateful, too," Murrin went on. "This Boston man is. And smart enough to know he needs a practical cow-country partner. That's why he'll sign over a clean third interest to Russ Hyatt, making him manager and range boss."

A cheer broke from the crowd. And a smile widened Murrin's face as he added: "Of course, this Boston man's feeling pretty good right about now. Like a man always does when the right girl says yes."

"Gettin' married, is he, Luke?" a man prompted. "Who is she?"

Colonel Murrin silenced him with a look. Naturally he didn't answer. His code was that a lady must never be mentioned by name at a bar.

But for Russ Hyatt, no name was needed. So that was it! He should have guessed it himself. He remembered Cort and Jean Markle coming hand-in-hand across the lobby, Cort with a self-conscious grin on his face. How much more, Russ wondered, had happened while he was off in the hills with Skeets Carson?

A customer was saying: "They was a lot of bawlin' down at the shippin' pens as I rode by, Luke. Sounded like a full trainload. Who's shippin'?"

Again Murrin proved he saw all, heard all, knew all. "The Scottish-American Ranch Company, Limited," he answered promptly. "They're rushing thirty cars to Chicago to pick up some quick dividend money. Idea's to reassure stockholders in Scotland when they hear about the Grimes tally. Nothing soothes an investor's nerves better than a fast dividend check."

"How far do you figure the market'll drop, Luke?"

Murrin shot his cuffs with their monogrammed

buttons, closed his eyes shrewdly. "Not much below four cents," he hazarded. "I always said it will take *two* shocks to bust Wyoming. A big tally-book scandal and the worst blizzard in history. We've had the scandal—but the big freeze is still to come. Let's hope it *never* comes. Step up to the bar, gentlemen; next one's on the house."

Still unnoticed, Russ slipped quietly out to his horse.

He stepped into the saddle and took off at a lope. At Dyer's Hotel he turned south on Eddy. A man coming out of Wes Moyer's Club called to him but Russ loped on, single-purposed. For Luke Murrin after all had given him an idea about where to find Lorton.

A cattle train was leaving for Chicago! How better could Lorton get clear of Cheyenne?

The next passenger train wasn't due through till after daylight. Lorton would expect the law to be at the depot to see if he'd take it. But a long dark freight train, leaving just after midnight, might not be searched.

Russ loped on to Fifteenth Street and there he turned toward the shipping pens. He could hear the bawling of carred cattle, the bump of couplings as a train was being made up.

Dark blanketed the yards except for the tail-lights of a caboose, and a swinging lantern here and there. Russ came opposite the caboose just as it was bunted onto a long string of stock cars. A brakeman whirled his lantern, yelling: "That does it, Ed. Put on the coffee and let's roll."

Russ tied the buckskin by a switchman's shanty and ran across half a dozen tracks to the caboose. A quick look into it told him Lorton wasn't there. He'd be more likely to ride the rods or perch on a coupling between cars.

The thirty cars strung out toward an engine, easterly up the track. Russ hurried that way, stooping to look under each car as he passed. Bawling steers made a constant din from end to end of the train.

Starlight was barely enough to let him see rods under the cars. Yet he'd make out the shape of a man, if Lorton was clinging there. The man wouldn't dare hide in a close-packed cattle car for fear of being trampled.

Russ patrolled patiently all the way to the engine, finding no one either on rods or couplings. At the engine a fireman saw the shine of his badge and took him for one of Nolan's constables.

"Lookin' for tramps? They hardly ever ride a stock train. Skeered to get in with the cattle. They'd rather wait for a hay train where they can bed down snug." The fireman turned to his engineer. "Ed's givin' us the highball, Boss."

The engine tooted twice and couplings clashed, taking up slack through the train. The shipment of steers began moving. Russ stood indecisive for a moment, letting the first two cars go by. Then he caught hold of iron rungs on the third car, swinging himself up. Lorton could be on a car roof. Russ went on up the ladder to the car's top.

It was flat and deserted, with a two-foot catwalk down its middle. Russ faced toward the rear of the train but in the darkness he could only see two or three car-lengths away. The train moved under him, slowly, jolting over frogs. It stopped for a switch to be thrown ahead, and the sudden buckle threw Russ off balance. He righted himself and began running down the car roofs toward the caboose.

Every forty feet he had to jump a gap to the next car. Always he could see dimly down the next several car-lengths, but no farther. As far as he could see them the roofs were bare. Again a sudden jerk unbalanced him. The train was moving again, grinding noisily through a switch.

Russ kept running on, jumping from car to car. He'd have to hurry because soon the train would be on the main line speeding toward Nebraska. Cattle stirred and bawled under him as the wheels bumped over switch points. Russ leaped another dark gap and raced on, the range of his sight reaching only a few bare roofs ahead.

Still the train bumped on slowly east, while Russ ran precariously west down the roofs.

Unless he finished before the train picked up speed, he'd have trouble getting off. He jumped another gap . . . then another. At the end of each car was a rod and brake wheel. How far to the caboose? Maybe after all he should have tried the livery barns . . .

Indistinctly, two car-lengths ahead, he saw someone sitting on a brake wheel. The shape of a man wearing a sheepskin coat with a turned-up collar. It could be a brakeman . . . or a tramp . . . or Gerald Lorton!

Russ stopped, drew his forty-five. The bawling of cattle rang in discord with a crackle of wheels, and a pungent, fleshy smell came up from below. If that man was a brakeman, why didn't he sing out a challenge?

A jar of the train made Russ throw out an arm for balance. Then he moved slowly forward, down the roof catwalk, gun level.

22

The shape two lengths away stood up. Otherwise it didn't move. One of its hands clung to a brake wheel. In the gloom Russ couldn't see whether the other held a gun. He advanced to the rear of his own car and called out, "Going anywhere, Lorton?"

A shot came from Lorton and then Russ heard the click of a breech bolt. Dimly he could see Lorton holding a short rifle, stock at cheek. The man fired again from a car-length away and only the jolts of a moving train saved Russ. Russ fired his own gun once, hardly hoping for a hit. Again a bolt clicked and again Lorton fired at him. *Three,* Russ counted.

He stood erect and still, wasting no more shots of his own. *Four,* he counted, as the best rifleman in Wyoming fired again at a range of forty-odd feet. But light was dim and always the train was moving, swaying, jolting over a ladder of switch points and frogs.

Russ saw Lorton jump to the car behind him and run rearward to the next brake wheel. There he turned to fire again. *Five,* Russ counted.

And Lorton could only fire once more without reloading. His carbine was sure to be the new 45-70 Hotchkiss repeater. Six shots was its limit, one in the chamber and five in the magazine. "A warrant for you, Lou," Russ shouted. He jumped to the next car and ran its length. It put him again only a car away from Lorton.

All the while the cars jolted, buckled, bumped. A hit would be an accident, even with a rifle held by an expert like Lorton. "You want to give up, Lou? Or would you rather shoot it out?"

It did what he hoped for—drew a sixth shot from Lorton.

Russ jumped one more gap and ran down the next roof, his gun aimed and cocked. Against the blur of night he saw Lorton frantically reloading, cramming shells into magazine and chamber. "You haven't got time, Lou." Russ covered the last few steps and was there, pushing his gun into Lorton's middle.

Lorton swore at him and clubbed the half-loaded rifle to swing it at Hyatt's head. Russ ducked under the swing and came up with a grip on Lorton's wrist. He twisted with a torturing torsion until the carbine fell, dropping between cars to clang on a coupling.

A brakeman yelled from the dark. "What's going on?" He was racing down the roofs from the caboose. With grinds and jerks the cattle train stopped.

"End of the line, Lou," Russ said. A great weariness came over him. He was glad when the freight crew helped him get Lorton down the car ladder.

Walking Lorton back to the switchman's shanty wearied him still more. There Russ untied the Y Bar buckskin but didn't dare mount. He kept his gun at the small of Lorton's back and took no chances. "Hep, Lou. Next stop's the courthouse."

His right hand held the gun and his left the reins of his horse. Leading the horse he prodded Lorton along Fifteenth, keeping to the middle of the street. It made less chance for the man to dodge up some alley in the dark.

The freight yard shots had been heard and rumors were flying. Customers tumbled out of Strom's saloon and from the Metropolitan bar. They lined up along the walk, gaping as Russ marched by with Lorton.

At Ferguson Russ turned north, still keeping to the middle of the street. It was an hour after midnight but saloons and hotels were alive and lighted. Men poured out of the Leighton House as Russ reached Sixteenth. Awed talk swept along the walks. "That's him!" "You don't mean Hyatt?" "Who else? That there's the same buckskin bronc what gave us the tip-off on Grimes!"

No one came nearer than the walks. Russ had the street all to himself and by the time he got to the Gold Room he was in a lane between gawking galleries. Every game stopped at the Gold Room. Across at the Delta Club even the dealers came out to watch a two-man parade up Ferguson. Two men and a buckskin horse.

From there the galleries began moving with Russ, keeping even with him and buzzing with talk. "It's Hyatt, all right. He was on that same bronc, couple of hours ago, when he cut down Grimes." "Who's the guy he's proddin' along?" "It ain't Grimes. Grimes done took *his* walk tonight." "Who you got there, Hyatt?"

Russ gave them no answers. He crossed Seventeenth and kept on, the Carey Block at his left and on his right the dark, lumber-piled lot where he'd shot it out with Idaho Brown.

From here on there were no saloons and the street darkened. At Eighteenth he could barely see the ivy-coated brick which was St. Mark's Church. Nor the roller-skating rink just beyond.

But across Nineteenth the courthouse still had its lower windows lighted. "This is where you live, Lou." Russ punched Lorton with his gun, hustling him up the courthouse steps.

"New boarder, Frank," he announced to the night jailer. "Name's Lou. If you're crowded, we can put him in with Grimes."

When Russ came out to his horse most of the crowd had drifted off to the saloons. He was swinging a tired leg over the saddle when he saw Miles Cortney. Cortney stepped off the walk and stood at his stirrup. "Been trying to catch up with you all evening, Russ."

Russ grinned down at him. "I already heard the good news, Cort. About you and Jean. Where you gonna set up housekeepin'? Boston or New York?"

"Neither. Our address'll be the Boxed M ranch, as soon as I bid it in. Which reminds me, Russ, I want you to do me a favor."

"Just name it, Cort."

"You wouldn't turn me down, would you? Promise?"

"Not in a million years, fella. Anything you say goes."

"Then it's all settled, podnah." Cortney's boyish smile and his drawled accent on the last word jerked Hyatt's mind back to what he'd heard at Murrin's bar. "I want you to accept a third interest in the layout. Land and cattle." Cortney held up a hand as Russ started to protest. "You promised. So don't try to run out on me. Anyway I'd go broke without you to run things out there. Right now you'd better put away your horse and get some sleep. See you at the hotel." With a wave of his unbandaged arm the Boston man cocked his big Western hat to a slant and set off down Ferguson.

Russ looked after him with a tightness in his throat. Then he rode west along Nineteenth, heading for the IXL stable.

After a block he came to the dark deserted corner where four weeks ago tonight they'd hung

Mosier, and where tonight they'd all but hung Grimes.

Looking up at a telegraph pole's crossarm brought a shiver to Russ. The mob had left half the rope draped over it. Only a moment ago something fine and clean had touched Russ—the warm, loyal generosity of Miles Cortney. Here in brutal contrast was something ugly and sordid. "The Shame of Cheyenne," Jean Markle called it. And that jail cage was another. The vice-ridden West End, into which he was now riding, was still another. All the ugliness of Cheyenne had rubbed against him tonight.

An impulse to get away from it made him rein to the right and head up Eddy to Twentieth. There he turned east, aimlessly, impelled toward the beauty of Cheyenne and away from its shame. For beauty and decency *were* here, sleeping behind lilacs and picketed lawns. Churches and schools were here, and people like the Garrisons. . . .

At the Hill Street corner he saw Gail's tall, many-gabled house, dark and shuttered and deep on its fountained lawn. She'd gone in and to bed long ago, he supposed. But he stopped the buckskin in front of her gate and sat hunched in the saddle, looking up at the dark windows, wondering which was Gail's.

A good thing she couldn't see him! He felt dirty and haggard. The smell of a cattle train was on him and the stench of the county jail. Yet still he sat there, half dreaming, hooking a leg around his saddle horn to roll a cigaret. Here it was clean and cool and decent and someday all of Cheyenne would be that way. Women like Gail Garrison and Jean Markle would rub out its sordid shadows and make it beautiful.

He sucked on the cigaret and relaxed, pushing from his mind every scene of the night except this one. He forgot about Grimes and Lorton, and even about Skeets and Cort. His thoughts just now had no room for anything except a girl who lived in this dark, sleeping house.

Its door opened and suddenly she was there. A girl in a long, dark cloak came out and walked swiftly along the brick path to the gate.

"I looked out and saw you, Russ."

The starlight on her face held him spellbound.

"What happened, Russ?" Her question was warm and frankly eager. When he still didn't answer she asked it again. "Can't you tell me anything at all?"

He stepped to the ground and crossed the walk. Only the gate was between them. "I could tell you a lot, Gail. Mostly it's about how beautiful you are. And about how much time I fritter away thinking about you. But right now it's late. Too late to be keeping you up."

She opened the gate and came out on the walk.

She looked up at him and said softly, "Tell me now, Russ Hyatt."

He took her cheeks between his hands and kissed her gently on the lips. The words he wanted to say didn't come out, so he kissed her again.

There was no hurry now. Time was forever and they both knew it. Even the buckskin horse seemed to know it. It stood hipshot and cock-kneed, reins hanging, patiently waiting.

Center Point Large Print
600 Brooks Road / PO Box 1
Thorndike, ME 04986-0001 USA

(207) 568-3717

US & Canada:
1 800 929-9108
www.centerpointlargeprint.com